THE BEAST WITHIN

THE BEAST WITHIN
A TALE OF BEAUTY'S PRINCE

BY SERENA VALENTINO

Bath · New York · Cologne · Melbourne · Delhi
Hong Kong · Shenzhen · Singapore

This edition published by Parragon Books Ltd in 2016

Parragon Books Ltd
Chartist House
15–17 Trim Street
Bath BA1 1HA, UK
www.parragon.com

Written by Serena Valentino
Adapted in part from Disney's *Beauty and the Beast*

ISBN 978-1-4748-4081-1

Printed in Italy

Dedicated to my dearest love, Shane Case
– Serena Valentino

CHAPTER I

THE WITCHES IN THE ROSE GARDEN

The Beast stood in his rose garden, the overwhelming scent of new blossoms making him slightly dizzy. His garden always seemed to have a life of its own, as if the twisting thorny vines could wrap themselves round his racing heart and put an end to his anxiety. There were times when he wished they would, but now his mind was filled with images of the beautiful young woman inside his castle: Belle, so brave and noble – willing to take her father's place as a prisoner in the castle dungeon. What sort of woman would do that – give up her life so easily, sacrificing her freedom for her father's? The Beast wondered if he was capable of such a sacrifice. He wondered if he was capable of love.

THE BEAST WITHIN

He stood there looking at the view of his castle. He tried to recall how the castle had looked before the curse. It was different now – menacing, and alive. Even the spires of his castle seemed to consciously pierce the sky with a violent fervour. He could only imagine how the place looked from a distance. It was tall and imposing and perched on the top of the highest mountain in the kingdom, and it appeared as though it were cut from the very mountain itself, surrounded by a thick green forest filled with dangerous wild creatures.

Only since he had been forced to spend his life hidden within its wretched walls and on its grounds had he done such things as take in his surroundings this way – actually see and, indeed, *feel* them. He now contemplated the moonlight casting sinister shadows on the statues that flanked the path leading from the castle to his garden – large winged creatures more frightening than anything from the ancient stories the tutors of his youth had made him study. He couldn't recall these sculptures being there before the castle and its lands were enchanted.

There had been many changes since the witches had brought their enchantments. The topiaries, for example, seemed to snarl at him as he prowled the labyrinth on evenings like this, attempting to take his mind off his troubles.

He had long since got used to the statues' watchful eyes glancing at him when he wasn't looking at them directly – and their slight movements he caught only out of the corner of his eye. He couldn't escape the feeling of being watched, and had almost got used to it. Almost. And the grand entrance of his castle seemed to him like a gaping mouth prepared to devour him. He spent as much time outdoors as possible. The castle felt like a prison, and as large as it was it confined him, choking the life out of him.

Once, when he was still – dare he think it! – *human*, he spent much of his time outdoors, stalking wild beasts in his forests for sport. But when he himself turned into something to be hunted, he shut himself away in those first years, never leaving the West Wing, let alone the castle.

Perhaps that was why he now detested being indoors: he had once spent so much time locked away by his own fear.

When the castle was first enchanted, he thought that his mind was playing tricks on him – that simply the idea of the curse had driven him mad. But he now knew everything that surrounded him was alive, and he was fearful any further misdeeds on his part would send it into a frenzy, and his enemies would make him suffer even more for the pain he had caused so many before he became a beast. The physical transformation was only part of the curse. There was much more, and it was far too frightening to think of.

Right now he wanted to think of the only thing that could calm him even slightly. He wanted to think of her.

Belle.

He looked upon the lake to the right of the garden, the moon creating beautiful silver patterns on the rippling water. Apart from his thoughts of Belle, this was the only tranquillity he had been afforded since the curse. He spent many hours here, careful not to catch sight of his own reflection, though sometimes he was tempted. He was fully aware of the revulsion it would bring.

He had been almost obsessed with his reflection when the curse began to take hold, and he quite liked the little changes in his appearance at first. The deep lines had made his young face more fearsome to his enemies, he had mused. But now ... now that the curse had overtaken him completely, he couldn't stand the sight of himself. Every mirror in the castle had been broken or shut away in the West Wing. His terrible deeds were engraved on his face, and that sent a hollow, wretched feeling deep into his gut, sickening him.

But enough of that.

He had a beautiful woman within his walls. She was a willing captive, someone to talk to, and yet he couldn't even bring himself to face her.

Fear.

It gripped him again. Would his fear now keep him outside, where once it had shut him *in*?

Fear of going inside and facing the girl? She was a wise woman. Had she no idea his fate was in *her* hands?

The statues watched, as they always did, when he heard the click of tiny boots on the stone path heading in his direction, disturbing his musings....

The odd sisters! Lucinda, Ruby and Martha, an indistinguishable trio of witches with inky-black ringlets, a milky pallor with the texture of bleached driftwood, and red baby-doll lips, were standing before him in his rose garden. Their faces were glowing in the moonlight like those of ghosts with mocking expressions. Their finery glittered like stardust in his dark garden while the plumage in their hair made their bird-like gestures all the more grotesque. There was a nervousness about them; they were seized by a constant series of little twitches and gestures, as if they were in continuous communication with each other even when they weren't speaking. They seemed to be taking measure of him. And he let them. He stood in silence, as he often did when they came to him, waiting for them to speak.

They appeared whenever they pleased and always without warning. Never mind it was his castle, and his gardens. He had long before given up on insisting that they appear at his will. He soon discovered his own desires were of no consequence to them.

Their laughs were shrill and seemed to mock the tiny glimmer of hope the witches detected within his dark and lonely heart. Lucinda was the first to speak, as was their custom. He couldn't help being transfixed by her face when she spoke to him. She looked like an odd doll come to life, with her porcelain skin and ratty clothes, and her unfaltering monotone voice only made the scene more macabre.

"So, you've captured yourself a pretty little thing at long last."

He didn't bother asking how they knew Belle had come to his castle. He had his theories on how they always seemed to know everything about him, but didn't care to share them with the sisters.

"We're surprised, Beast," said Martha, her pale blue eyes watery and globe-like.

"Yes, surprised," Ruby spat with an eerie wide grin animating her too-red lips morbidly, like a dead creature brought to life by evil incantations.

"We expected your condition to have progressed by now," said Lucinda, her head cocked slightly to the right while she looked at him. "We dreamed of you running in the wood hunting smaller prey."

Ruby continued. "We dreamed of hunters tracking you down."

Martha laughed and said, "Hunting you like the beast you are and mounting your head on the Huntsmen's Tavern wall."

"Why, you're even wearing clothes, we see. Holding on to the last shred of your humanity, is it?" they said in unison.

The Beast did nothing to betray his terror – terror not of the witches' magic but of his own threatening nature, of which they were reminding him. They were holding a mirror up to the monster within, which was longing to escape. It was a beast that wanted to kill the witches and everything else in its path. He longed to see blood and bones, to taste their flesh. If he tore at their throats with his claws, he'd never have to listen to their shrill taunting voices again.

Lucinda laughed.

"Now that is what we expected of you, Beast."

And Martha said, "He will never capture Belle's heart, Sister, no matter how desperate he is to break the curse."

"He's too far gone now, I daresay."

"Perhaps if he showed her how he once looked, she may have pity on him," Ruby said as a maddening cacophony of laughter filled the rose garden.

"Pity him, yes, but love him? Never!"

The Beast used to hurl insults back at all of them, but it seemed only to fuel their passion for cruelty, and he didn't dare stir up his own anger and desire for violence, so he just stood stock-still, waiting for their little torture session to end.

Martha spoke again. "In case you've forgotten, here are the rules, Beast, laid out by all the sisters: You must love her and that love must be returned with true love's kiss, before your 21st birthday.

She may use the mirror as you do, to see into the world beyond your kingdom, but she must never know the details of the curse or how it's to be broken. You will notice she sees the castle and its enchantments differently from you. The most terrifying aspects of the curse are reserved for you."

The Beast stared blankly at the witches.

Martha smiled creepily and continued. "This is your one advantage. The only thing in this castle or on its grounds that will frighten Belle is your visage."

Lucinda chimed in. "When was the last time you looked upon your reflection, Beast? Or saw to the rose?"

There had been a time when the rose wasn't out of his sight. Lately he tried to forget it. He had almost expected the sisters' visit this evening would be to inform him that the last petal had fallen off its enchanted stem. But they were just here to mock him, as always, to tempt him into violence, and they'd love nothing more than to see his soul further besmirched.

Lucinda's cackling voice brought him out of his reverie. "It won't be long now...."

Martha continued. "Not long at all, Beast."

"Soon the last petal will fall and you shall remain in this form with no chance of transformation to your former self."

"And on that day...."

"We will dance!" they finished in unison.

The Beast finally spoke. "And what of the others? Are they to remain as they are, doomed to enchantment as well?"

Ruby's eyes widened in wonder. "Concern? Is that what we detect? Isn't that odd?"

"Concern for himself."

"Yes, for himself, always himself, never others."

"Why would he concern himself with servants? He never gave them a second thought, unless it was to punish them."

"I think he's afraid of what they might do to him if he doesn't break the curse."

"I think you're right, Sister."

"I am also interested in seeing what they'll do."

11

"It shall be a gruesome spectacle indeed."

"And we shall take much pleasure in bearing witness to it."

"Don't forget, Beast, true love, both given and received, before the last petal falls."

And with that the sisters turned on the heels of their tiny pointed boots and clicked their way out of the rose garden, the sound fading little by little until they vanished into a sudden mist and the Beast could no longer hear them at all.

CHAPTER II

THE REFUSAL

The Beast sighed and slumped down on the stone bench in the shadow of the winged-creature statue hovering above him. Its shadow mingled with his own – his face and its wings – merging into what looked like a Shedu, the winged lion from ancient myth. It had been so long since he'd seen even his shadow that he hardly knew what he looked like, and this shadow stirred a great interest in him.

With an infusion of light the shadow faded into nothingness. Remaining was a new stark-white statue, wearing a passive expression. It was neither male nor female – not as far as he could surmise, anyway – and it was standing completely still with a small brass candelabrum in one hand, candles burning, while the other hand pointed towards the castle entrance. It was as if the stone figure was commanding him back to the castle, back into the gaping mouth.

He feared if he returned, the castle would at long last devour him.

He made his way back, leaving the silent statue and the sisters' taunting words in the garden. The light from the candelabrum looked tiny now, like fireflies in the distance.

The statue would make its way back to the castle in its own time, more than likely when the Beast was far enough away. They never moved or came to him while he was looking at them directly; they were always sneaking up on him while his attentions were elsewhere. It frightened him, really, to know they could come up to him at any time and do with him what they would, but that was yet another portion of the curse he had to contend with.

He thought about what the sisters had said, and he wondered how Belle saw the castle's enchantments and how its cursed servants appeared to her.

The Refusal

As he made his way through the foyer towards the dining room, he stopped to listen to the muted voices coming from Belle's chamber but couldn't quite make out what was being discussed. He was creeping down the hallway, hoping to get a peek at whom she was speaking to, when he heard a gentleman with a French accent inviting her to dine with the master of the house. She slammed her door and refused.

"I won't! I don't want anything to do with him! He's a monster!"

Monster! His anger got the better of him. "If she won't dine with me, then she won't eat at all," he growled, turning the corner and half expecting to see another of the living statues standing there to torment him, but the only evidence of anyone having been there at all was the small gold candelabrum he'd just seen in the rose garden, now extinguished, with a tiny ribbon of smoke curling up from the smouldering wick.

"She thinks I'm a monster!" he fumed.

He felt his anger mounting, raging out of control as he stormed his way to the West Wing.

Monster! His claws gouged the wooden banister as he went up the long stairway, wishing it was flesh and blood, not splintering wood.

Monster!

There was very little light in this part of the castle. It was completely dark apart from the moonlight that came through the tattered red curtains of his bedroom. Leaning on the far wall were stacks of different-shaped mirrors covered in white moth-eaten cloths. Among the mirrors were portraits, some of which had been destroyed by his anger and frustration, the visages mocking him as the witches had, taunting him with his former likeness.

Monster!

He couldn't light a fire in the staggeringly large fireplace or the torches on the wall brackets. His paws couldn't master tiny things like matches, and the servants weren't allowed into the West Wing. Not even the sisters came to this part of the castle. He had escaped their mockery for long stretches of time when he spent most of his days

16

here in the beginning – hiding away, letting his anger swell to epic proportions, fearful of what he was becoming, yet intrigued concurrently.

It had been that way at first, hadn't it? Intriguing. The subtle differences in his features, the lines round his eyes that frightened his foes when he narrowed them. Using a look rather than words to strike fear into his enemies had been very useful indeed.

He *had* looked upon himself in the mirror in those days, trying to distinguish which sorts of deeds caused the most horrific alterations in his appearance. Knowing that this was a degenerative curse that wouldn't abate.

The sisters seemed to know of his compulsion and teased him about it, saying he would suffer the fate of their cousin's second wife if he wasn't careful. The sisters were always talking nonsense, always speaking in fragments, and suffered from fits of laughter so severe he hardly knew what they were on about most of the time. He was not sure even they were aware. Could it all be the ramblings of maddened minds? Here he was – taunted by insane crones. *He*, who had once been a prince.

Once. And now ... now he couldn't even venture out of his gardens or approach a wounded stranger who might wander from the forest to his castle in the night without sending him running in fear.

What did Belle think of what little she saw of him by dungeon torchlight? But he knew, didn't he? She'd called him a monster! Leave her to the servants, then; let them weave tales of his dastardly deeds! Let them confirm how vile and ugly he was. He cared not! After all, he was a monster. And monsters knew not feelings, especially the sentiment called *love*.

His anger and confusion were quelled as his head spun from exhaustion. He sat on the bed, wondering what to do next. The sisters implied that the girl was his only hope of escaping the curse. Liars! He could make her fall in love with him easily enough if he looked as he once had – handsome, well groomed, some might say arrogant.

Women were easily managed then. A few flowery words of love, feigning some interest in what she had to say, perhaps showing a pretence of vulnerability and the girl was his. And often he didn't even need to resort to such nonsense; only if the girl was exceedingly beautiful would he bother to try to win her admiration. Typically, his looks alone were enough to catch them spellbound.

But the way he looked now.... He had no idea how to go about this with Belle. He pushed himself on to his feet, feeling the rough and tattered sheets with the pads of his paws. Perhaps he *should* let servants in to make the bed, dust the windows and mop the floors. To have him live more like a human being than the monster he had become.

He stood on shaking legs, still dizzy from the rush of animal anger he'd felt when he heard Belle call him a monster. He moved to the mantel, where he kept the enchanted mirror the sisters had given him long before. He stood there for a moment, taking a deep breath before he looked at himself. It had been far too long since he had seen his own reflection. He had to see how his odious deeds had etched themselves upon his face.

His paw rested on the sheet that was draped over the frame. Then, in one movement, he tore the sheet away and tossed it aside, revealing the looking glass and the tarnished reflection that stared back at him.

Monster!

The only indication of what he had once been was his soulful blue eyes, which teemed with humanity. Those hadn't changed. They were still his.

But in all other respects, he had become exactly what he had feared. And, indeed, it was worse than he ever could have fathomed.

His knees buckled as his world started to close in. His scope became narrower until he found himself in utter darkness, spiralling into a vision of his past – of himself as he'd once been, before he became a monster. Before he became the Beast.

CHAPTER III

THE PRINCE

Before the curse, life had been good to the Prince.

To hear the sisters tell the tale of the curse would be to hear a story filled with examples of what a terrible person he was, a list of his misdeeds, tallied one by one, each of them worse and nastier than the one before, until the sisters swooped down on him with their spell, deforming him into the pathetic beast now lying on his bedroom floor before the mirror.

Eventually, that is indeed how the story will go. But the sisters won't be able to spew that part of the tale at first. Not until the Prince has had his say, a chance to tell you how much fun he had.

Because there was once a time when things were good.

It was a time when the Prince was just an arrogant young man, full of pride and keenly aware of his station in life. What young prince hasn't found himself in exactly the same place? What do you think other princes are like? Are they just charming men venturing off hither and thither in search of sleeping brides to awaken with love's first kiss? Do you fancy them as dandy gentlemen while they slay dragons and vanquish foul, murderous stepmothers? Perhaps they do that sort of thing without the slightest bit of ego or aggression? One moment they're hacking their way through enchanted killer thornbushes only to find a fire-breathing dragon primed for murder on the other side, and the next they're expected to waltz with their brides in pastel suits and golden sashes.

And what is up with those sashes, anyway? Horrible!

Our prince didn't want anything to do with that romantic poppycock. He wanted a different life,

and he learned early on he didn't have to slay
a fire-breathing beast to get a fair maiden to kiss
him. Though swaggering in with the corpse of a
giant elk or a fearsome grizzly bear slung over his
shoulder for Old Man Higgins to stuff and mount
on the tavern wall did get him his fair share of
smooches from the young ladies – and as dangerous
as it might have been at times, it was a far cry
from poison apples, stinky dwarfs or being burned
alive by an evil fairy queen. He'd take hunting and
philandering over that stuff any day.

Life was good; everyone loved and worshipped
the Prince and he knew it.

As he sat in a tavern, his clothes covered
in earth, grime and the blood from his
latest kill, he couldn't have been more handsome.
Or at least that was what he thought. The tavern
was his favourite haunt. It had almost everything
he loved in one place. The wood walls were so
crowded with the forest beasts he'd slain that
Old Man Higgins laughed and teased him as he
poured him another beer.

"I'm going to have to build a larger tavern, my Prince!"

And it was true.

The only person who killed almost as many animals as the Prince was his good friend Gaston, who slammed a handful of coins on to the bar, startling poor Higgins before he could finish pouring the new round of drinks. "Drinks are on me tonight, Higgins! In celebration of the Prince's engagement!"

The men cheered and the barmaids wilted into tears, their bosoms heaving heavy sighs of disappointment. Gaston seemed to enjoy the spectacle as much as the Prince did.

"She is the most beautiful girl in the village! You're a lucky man! I'd be jealous if you weren't the very best of my friends!"

That he was. Gaston's best friend.

They had always been alike, Gaston and the Prince, and the Prince supposed that was why they had enjoyed each other's company so well. Or perhaps he had felt it was better to keep his competition close at hand. But then again, he wondered if that was how he'd actually seen it then.

The Prince couldn't help laughing sometimes while listening to Gaston go on about himself, bragging about his cleft chin, showing off his hairy chest, and singing his own praises up and down the town's main thoroughfares.

However, there was another side to the Prince's old friend, a vindictive cruelty about him.

Yes, they were very much alike, Gaston and the Prince, and that is what brought them together.

Gaston was the first to let the Prince know his fiancée, Circe, was from a poor farming family, in an attempt to prevent the Prince from shaming himself by marrying someone so low. *Of course* he couldn't marry her, no matter how beautiful she was. How could his subjects take the daughter of a pig farmer seriously as their queen? The servants wouldn't respect her, and she wouldn't know how to act in diplomatic situations. No, it would be a disaster. It would be unfair to his subjects and to her, and most of all to him. He didn't need anyone to tell him it was a poor idea; he came to the conclusion himself the moment he discovered her station in life.

Then the decision was made.

He couldn't marry the girl.

The Prince sent for his fiancée the next day. Circe looked beautiful when she stepped out of the carriage to meet him. Her light blonde hair and shimmering silver dress glistened under the morning sun as she stood in his rose garden. It was hard to believe she was a pig farmer's daughter. Perhaps Gaston was mistaken. Where would a girl on a pig farm get a dress like that? Ah. Gaston was playing his tricks again. Trying to put him off so he could have Circe for himself. That wicked bum-chinned brute. He would have words with him about this soon enough. But in the meantime he had to make amends with his beautiful Circe. Of course she had no idea he had intended to break things off, but he felt his heart had betrayed her.

"My darling, Circe, you look beautiful."

She looked up at him with her pale blue eyes, with a slight blush that did not diminish the light smattering of freckles across her button nose.

Adorable.

She was simply that, adorable. How could he have thought she was the daughter of a pig farmer? He couldn't fathom her mucking about with those dirty, horrible creatures.

Think of it! Circe feeding pigs! It was laughable when he saw her sparkling like a dew-dropped rose, like the princess she was about to become. He would make Gaston pay for causing him to doubt her.

"Come, my love, to the morning room. I have arranged something special just for you."

He didn't mention Gaston's trick to Circe; it was too nasty to repeat. There was no need to cause ill will between the two. Gaston would, after all, be his best man at the wedding. Yes, he was brutish, ill-tempered and conniving, but he was still his closest companion. And he wanted his best friend to stand beside him at his wedding.

And there was something else. It would please the Prince to know Gaston would be seething with envy as he stood there, forced to watch the wedding proceedings, knowing his attempts to break the Prince's faith in Circe had failed and he could not have her for himself. Yes, that would be very satisfying. Perhaps after the wedding he should send Gaston away on some errand for the kingdom – something distasteful and below his rank, to show him not to interfere again.

Who could blame Gaston, really, for trying to spirit Circe away from him? She was the prettiest girl they'd ever seen, and Gaston was only giving in to her beauty and letting it taint his better judgement. It was quite funny when you thought about it – Gaston, the prince of Bum-chin-land, trying to take his Circe away! Who would have a commoner, no matter how close a royal family friend he might be, when she could have the prince who would one day be king of these lands?

The Prince decided to laugh the entire thing off and focus on what he loved: hunting, drinking, spending the taxes collected from his estates and charming the ladies.

Oh yes, and there was Circe, but he loved her the way one would love his castle, or his stable stocked with the finest horses. She was the most beautiful creature, and he treasured her for how her beauty would reflect on him and his kingdom. Sensible, he thought, and he felt beyond reproach.

The wedding plans continued even though Gaston kept on about Circe's family. Not a day or night went by that he didn't mention it.

"You're starting to bore me, Gaston, honestly! Going on about this pig-farm thing as if it were actually true. Why don't you give up already?"

Gaston wouldn't let the issue alone.

"Come with me, good friend, I will show you!"

So they rode several kilometres, until they reached the little farmhouse, which was tucked away beyond the woods on an uncommon path.

There was his Circe. She was standing in the pen feeding the pigs, the bottom of her simple white dress caked with mud. Her hair seemed dull, and her cheeks were flushed with hard work. She must have sensed them looking at her, for she glanced up and noticed the expression of disgust on her beloved's face, leaving her stricken with horror and shame.

She dropped her pail and stood on the spot, looking at the two men.

She said nothing.

"Come out here, girl! Is that how you greet your guests?" the Prince barked cockily.

Her eyes widened as if she was coming out of a haze.

"Of course," she said timidly.

Then she walked out of the pen and approached the men, looking up at them, still astride their horses. She felt small and meek and unable to meet their disapproving gazes.

"Hello, my love, what brings you here?" she asked.

The Prince scoffed rudely. "What brings me indeed? Why didn't you tell me your father was a mere pig farmer?"

Circe looked desperate and confused, hardly able to answer.

"What do you mean, my dearest?"

The Prince was enraged. "Do not play coy with me, madam! How dare you keep such a thing from me! How could you lie to me in such a manner?"

Circe crumpled in tears. "You never asked about my parents! I never lied to you! Why should it matter? We love each other! And love conquers all."

"Love *you*? Seriously? Look at yourself – covered in muck! How could I *possibly* love you?"

He spat on the ground and then turned his attentions to his friend. "Come on, Gaston, let's leave this stinking place. I have nothing further to say to this filthy farm girl."

And the two men rode off, leaving the beautiful maiden covered in mud and a cloud of dust kicked up by their wild horses.

CHAPTER IV

THE WITCHES' LITTLE SISTER

The Prince sat alone in his study, sipping a drink by the fireplace. Images of Circe haunted him. They flashed between the bewitching young beautiful woman he wanted to marry and the sickening scene he'd witnessed earlier that day.

He almost felt sorry for her.

Almost.

But he could not soften to her, not after she had tried to trap him into marriage by weaving such horrid lies. As he sat there, sinister shadows danced on the walls. These were created by the firelight and the giant antlers mounted on the wall above his chair. He remembered the day he'd killed the largest trophy – the great elk. He had almost been sad the day he finally took him down. He'd been tracking the beast for years. But when he'd killed him, he felt as if he'd lost an old friend. He sipped some more, remembering that hallowed day. Just then the porter poked his head into the room.

"Prince, sir, Miss Circe is here to see you."

The Prince sighed with annoyance. "I've told you, numerous times now, not to admit her! Send her away!" And he turned back to his musings.

The porter didn't leave. He stuttered his reply. "I haven't le-le-let her in, m-my lord; she is standing outside, but refuses to-to-to go. She says she will not leave until you speak with her."

"Very well, then."

Putting his drink on the little wooden side table next to his chair, he stood with a heavy sigh and made his way towards the grand entrance.

There stood Circe, a pathetic little creature holding a single red rose and looking downright diminutive in the gaping arched doorway. Her eyes were sad, swollen and red from crying.

She looked nothing like the ravishing beauty that had once stood in his rose garden all gold, silver and light. If seeing her mucking around in the mud that day hadn't vanquished that memory from his mind, then this encounter most surely would.

He'd never again be tempted by memories of her beauty, trying to fool him into feeling sorry for the lying little creature! She had a ratty shawl round her shoulders that made her look like an old beggar woman. The light and shadow on her face made her look old and haggard. Had he not known it was her, he would have thought her an old beggar woman indeed.

She spoke with a small voice. She sounded like a little crow – her voice scratchy and hoarse from long crying.

"My love, please, I can't believe you would treat me so poorly. Surely you didn't mean the things you said to me earlier today."

She broke down sobbing, her tear-stained and swollen face buried in her small white hands.

How could he ever have thought her adorable?

"I cannot marry you, Circe. You must have known that from the start. I'm guessing that is why you tried to keep your parents a secret."

"But I didn't know, my love! My darling, please take this rose and remember the days you still loved me. Won't you please let me come inside, away from this cold? Do you hate me so much?"

"Your beauty, which so captured my heart in my very garden, will forever be tarnished by the *grotesque* scene I witnessed today, and by *this* shameful display."

When Circe's shawl fell back, the Prince was startled to see, her eyes were no longer swollen and her face was not splotched and red from long hours of crying. Her skin was pale and glowing as if she were infused with moonlight – and her hair was bright and shimmering with little silver adornments, like sparkling bits of stardust were captured within. Her dress was opalescent silver, and everything about her seemed to glow with enchantment, but nothing shined brighter than her pale blue eyes. She had never looked so beautiful.

"I'll never be quite as beautiful again in your eyes because you think I'm the daughter of a pig farmer?"

Then he heard their voices, climbing out of the darkness, like a chorus of harpies swooping up from Hell.

"Farmer's daughter?"

"Our little sister?"

"She is of royal blood, and cousin to the old king."

He couldn't see who was speaking; he only heard three distinct voices coming from the darkness. Something about the voices unnerved him. No, if he were completely honest with himself, he would admit the voices frightened him. He wanted nothing more than to slam the door and hide within the walls of his castle, but he stood his ground.

"Is this *true*, Circe?" he asked.

"Yes, my prince, it is. My sisters and I come from a long line of royalty."

"I don't understand!"

Circe's sisters stepped into the light and stood behind her. Their grotesquerie made Circe's beauty even more pronounced.

It was startling, really.

It wasn't that they were ugly, the sisters; it was just that everything about them was so striking, and in such contrast to their other features. Each feature on its own could have been beautiful. Their large eyes, for example, might have looked stunning on another woman. Their hair, somehow it was too black, like one could become lost in the depth of its darkness, and the contrast of their blood-red lips against their parchment-white skin was just too shocking. They didn't seem real, these sisters. None of this did, because all of it was absurd. He felt as if he must be dreaming, caught in a nightmare. He was entranced by Circe's transfiguration, and it made him forget his earlier vow never again to think of her.

He was enamoured with her beauty once more.

"Circe! This is *wonderful*! All is well, you're of royal descent, we can be married!"

"We had to be sure you really loved her," said Lucinda, her eyes narrowing.

"Yes, sure," said Martha.

"We wouldn't just –"

"Let our little sister marry a –"

"Monster!" they shouted accusingly in unison.

"Monster? How dare you!" the Prince snapped.

The sisters laughed.

"That is what we see –"

"A monster."

"Oh, others may find you handsome enough –"

"But you have a cruel heart!"

"And that's what *we* see, the ugliness of your soul."

"Soon *all* will see you for the cruel beast you are!"

"Sisters, *please*! Let me speak! He is mine, after all!" said Circe, trying to calm her sisters. "It is my right to deliver the retribution."

"There is no need for this," the Prince said, finally showing his fear – whether it be of the sisters or of losing the beautiful vision before him. "We can be married now. I've never seen a woman as beautiful as you. There's nothing to stand in our way. I *must* have you as my wife!"

"Your *wife*? Never! I see now you only loved my beauty. I will ensure no woman will ever want you no matter how you try to charm her! Not as long as you remain as you are – tainted by vain cruelty."

The sisters' laugh could be heard clear across the land on that night. It was so piercing that it sent hundreds of birds into flight and frightened the entire population of the kingdom, even Gaston. But Circe continued with her curse while Gaston and the others wondered what ominous happenings might be afoot.

"Your ugly deeds will mar that handsome face of yours, and soon, as my sisters said, everyone will see you as the beast you are."

She then handed the Prince the single rose she had tried to give him earlier. "And since you would not take this token of love from the woman you professed to cherish, let it then be a symbol of your doom!"

"*Your* doom!" Martha cried, laughing while she clapped her little white hands and hopped in her tiny boots with absolute glee.

"*Your* doom!" joined in Ruby and Lucinda, also jumping up and down, making the scene even more confusing and macabre.

"Sisters!" Circe pleaded. "I am not finished!"

She continued. "As the rose petals fall, so shall the years pass until your 21st birthday. If you have not found love – *true* love, both given and received – by that day, and sealed with a kiss, then you shall remain the horrifying creature you'll become."

The Prince squinted his eyes and cocked his head, desperately trying to comprehend the meaning of this riddle.

"Oh, he'll become the Beast! He will!"

"No doubt! He'll never change his wicked ways!"

The sisters were again clapping and jumping in vindictive delight. Their laughter seemed to feed upon itself. The more they laughed, the louder it became, and the more insane the sisters seemed to be. Circe had to take them in hand once again.

"Sisters, stop! He has to know the terms of the curse or it will not be binding."

The sisters' laughter ceased at once, and they became unnervingly quiet, twitching with discomfort.

"Mustn't ruin his punishment!"

"No, mustn't do that!"

Circe, hearing her sisters' chatter again, gave them a reproachful look, silencing them immediately.

"Thank you, Sisters. Now, Prince, do you understand the terms of the curse?" The Prince could only look at the women in wonder and horror.

"He's struck dumb, little sister!" cackled Lucinda.

"Shhh," reminded Ruby as Circe continued.

"Do you understand the terms, Prince?" she asked him again.

"That I'm supposed to turn into some sort of beast if I do not change my ways?" the Prince said, trying to repress a smile.

Circe nodded.

Now it was time for the Prince to laugh. "Poppycock! What sort of trickery is this? I'm to believe you've *cursed* me? Am I supposed to become so frightened that I fool myself into making something dreadful happen? I won't fall for it, ladies! If indeed you can be *called* ladies, royal blood or not!"

Circe's face hardened. The Prince had never seen her like this – so angry, so stern and cold.

"Your castle and its grounds shall also be cursed, then, and everyone within will be forced to share your burden. Nothing but horrors will surround you, from when you look into a mirror to when you sit in your beloved rose garden."

Lucinda added, "And soon those horrors will be your only scenery."

"Yes, I see you stuck cowering indoors."

"Yes, fearful of leaving your own bedchamber!"

"Yes, yes! Too frightened to show your ugly face to the world outside your castle walls!"

"I see your servants seething with hate, watching your every move from distant shadows, sneaking up on you in the night, just looking at the creature you've become."

"And I see *you*," Lucinda said, "wondering if they'll kill you to free themselves from the curse!"

"Enough! That is but one path he may take! There is one last thing he needs before we go."

Circe looked to Ruby. "The mirror, please."

Lucinda's face contorted even more freakishly than imaginable. "Circe, no! Not the mirror."

"It's our mirror!"

"Not yours to give away!"

"No, no, no!"

"This is *my* curse, Sisters, and on my terms. I say he gets the mirror!"

Circe continued. "My darling, this enchanted mirror will let you see into the outside world. All you need to do is ask the mirror and it will show you what you want to see."

"I don't like you giving away our treasures, Circe! That was a gift from a very famous maker of mirrors. It's quite priceless and very old. It's a mirror of legends! It was given to us before you were even born."

"And shall I remind you how you came to possess it?" asked Circe, silencing her sisters.

"Let's not bore the Prince with our family history, Circe," said Martha. "He can have the mirror, not only to see the outside world, but to see the hideous creature he's bound to become."

"Oh yes! Let him try to break the maidens' hearts after he's turned into the Beast!" screamed Ruby, with Lucinda and Martha chiming in,

"Let him try, let him try, to break their hearts and make them cry!" They were spinning in circles like toy tops, their dresses blossoming about them like mutant flowers in a strange garden, while they chanted their incessant mockery.

"Let him try! Let him try! To break their hearts and make them cry!"

Circe was growing impatient, and the Prince looked as if he was straddling amusement and fear.

"Sisters! Please stop, I beg you!" Circe snapped.

"I'm supposed to take this seriously? Any of this? Really, Circe! Do you think I'm an idiot like your cackling sisters here?"

Before the Prince could say any more, he found himself pressed firmly against the stone wall behind him, Circe's hand placed tightly round his throat, her voice a hiss like a giant serpent's.

"Never speak ill of my sisters again! And yes, you'd better take everything I've said seriously, and I suggest you commit it to memory, because your life depends on it. The curse is in your hands now. Choose the right path, Prince, change your ways, and you shall be redeemed. Choose cruelty and vanity and you will suffer indeed!"

She released him. He was utterly gobsmacked. Her face was very close to his and full of hate. He felt frightened, really frightened, perhaps for the first time in his young life.

"Do you understand?" she asked again vehemently, and all he could mutter was "Yes".

"Come, Sisters, let's leave him, then. He will choose his own path from here."

So he did.

CHAPTER V

THE PORTRAIT IN THE WEST WING

In the first few months there was no sign of a curse at all: no taunting sisters, no beastly visage and no villainous servants plotting his death. The whole idea was laughable, really. His loyal servants growing to hate him? Ludicrous! Imagine his beloved Cogsworth or doting Mrs Potts wishing for his death – utterly inconceivable! It was just pure claptrap!

Nothing of which the sisters spoke came true, and he saw no reason to believe it would. As a result, he did not think he needed to repent, change his ways or take anything those insane women had to say seriously at all.

Life went on and it was good – as good as it had always been, with Gaston at his side, money in his pockets and women to fawn over him. What more could he ask for?

But as happy as he was, he couldn't completely shake the fear that perhaps Circe and her sisters were right. He noticed little changes in his appearance – small things that made him feel his mind might be betraying him and he was somehow falling for the sisters' ruse.

He had to constantly – obsessively – remind himself that there was no curse. There were only his fears and the sisters' lies, and he wasn't about to let either get the better of him.

He was in his bedroom readying himself for a hunting trip with Gaston when the porter came in to let him know his friend had arrived.

"Send him up, then. Unless he wants to take his breakfast in the observatory while I finish getting ready."

The Prince was in fine spirits and found himself feeling better than he had in a long time.

But he couldn't remember the porter's name. A bit concerning, but one of the advantages of being a prince is that no one questions you. So if others were noticing a change in the Prince, they didn't mention it.

"Are my things packed? Is everything ready for our stalking expedition?" he asked the porter.

"Indeed, my liege, it's all been loaded. If there's nothing else that you require, then I shall see to the other gentleman's things?"

The Prince had to laugh. Gaston a gentleman? Hardly! The porter was too young to remember when Gaston and the Prince had been boys. Some of the older staff would remember. Mrs Potts would remember, to be sure. She had often recounted old stories about the boys as children, laughing at the memory of them running to the kitchen and pleading with her for sweets after their grand adventures, both of them covered in mud, tracking it throughout the castle, like little boys love to do, making a maid trail after them – a maid who muttered curses under her breath the entire time.

Curses.

Put them out of your mind. Remember something else.

Mrs Potts.

She loved telling the story of how the boys had convinced themselves the castle grounds had been plagued by an evil dragon. On more than one occasion, the boys went off adventuring all day and were gone well into the night, making everyone sick with worry over what might have befallen them – and the two of them just waltzed right in as happy and gay as could be, without a care in the world, wondering what the fuss was all about.

That was how those boys had been. The Prince wondered how much they'd actually changed, though Mrs Potts reminded him at every opportunity that both he and Gaston had changed a great deal. She often said she didn't see much of the little boys she once adored in either of them.

Changed.

He had changed, hadn't he? And not in the way Mrs Potts feared. In other ways. She still loved them, though. She couldn't help herself. She probably even thought of Gaston as a gentleman. She always treated him as such. She saw the best in everyone when she could, and encouraged their friendship when they were young, even though he was the gamekeeper's son.

"It shouldn't matter who his father is, young master. He is your friend and has proven to be a very good one at that." He remembered feeling terrible for letting a thing like status make him reconsider a friendship with Gaston. None of that mattered, not now. Gaston had his own lands and people to work them – the Prince had seen to that – and that life when they were so young, when Gaston lived with his father in the stable quarters, it all seemed so far away and long ago.

Gaston's very voice interrupted his thoughts.

"Prince! Why are you standing there daydreaming when you should be readying yourself? We have a long journey ahead of us."

"I was remembering when we were young, Gaston. Recalling our earlier adventures. Do you remember the time you saved my life in the...."

Gaston's face hardened. "You know I don't like to talk about that, Prince! Must you always remind me that I am not your equal?"

"That wasn't my aim, dear friend."

"Nevertheless, it is the *result*."

The Prince felt scolded.

Gaston seemed to be lost in his own thoughts now, musing over the large portrait of the Prince hanging over the fireplace. "When did you sit for this portrait? How long ago was it? Five years?"

"It was finished only a quarter of a year ago. You remember, it was done by that wildly eccentric painter. He called himself the Maestro, remember? He seemed to live in another world altogether with his pretty speeches about preserving our youth and making time stand still through the magic of depiction."

"I do! Yes, he was very ... uh, interesting."

"Interesting? You wanted to toss him out of the nearest window, if I recall!"

The two laughed but Gaston seemed to be preoccupied with thoughts other than those about strange painters and their proclamations of preserving a moment in time.

"I suppose there is something to his insane ramblings, though. I do seem much changed since this was painted. Look, around the eyes in the painting. There is no sign of lines, but if you see here, it does look as though I've aged more than five years."

"You sound like a woman, Prince, worrying about lines round the eyes! Next you'll be wondering what colour petticoat looks best with a blue dress. Shall I enquire with your fairy godmother?"

The Prince laughed, but it wasn't genuine. Gaston continued. "We have better things to do than waste the day clucking away like a couple of hens. Meet me in the observatory for breakfast when you're finished getting ready."

"Yes, feel free to start without me. I'm sure Mrs Potts is in a tizzy that it's taken us this long to get down there."

The portrait was still bothering him. How had his eyes become so lined in just a few months? Was it possible they had looked like this at the time and the painter wished to compliment him by making him seem younger? No, the Maestro was very specific about preserving that moment in time. Making it as pure and realistic as possible. Freezing a moment that could never be diminished or altered, keeping it for generations so it might evoke something of his memory once he was long gone. So the man had said, almost word for word. It seemed contrary to his annoying speeches and proclamations for him to have painted the Prince any differently than he had appeared at the time. So Gaston was right? Had he aged five years in just over three months? Or was Gaston simply being mean-spirited because he'd reminded him of when they were young?

Could it be? No. But what if ... what if Circe's curse was real?

Then he remembered the sisters' mirror. He had tucked it away the night the fiendish harpies gave it to him, and hadn't given it a second thought. Their words started to ring in his ears and he couldn't take his mind off the hellish thing.

The Beast Within

It will show you as the beast you are bound to become!
He walked over to the mantel. Sitting on top was a voluminous tortoiseshell cat with narrowed yellow eyes lined in black. She looked down on him, scrutinizing him as he looked for the button that opened the secret compartment within the fireplace mantel. The fireless pit was flanked by two griffons with ruby-red eyes that sparkled in the morning light.

He pressed one of the eyes inward, and it recessed into the griffon's skull. Each griffon had a crest on its chest; the crest on the griffon to the right popped out, revealing the compartment containing the mirror.

The Prince just stood there looking at it. The mirror had landed face down when he tossed it in. He stared at its back side. It was seemingly harmless, a simple silver hand mirror almost entirely black now from tarnish. He reached in, grabbing the mirror by its handle. It was cold in his hand, and he fancied he could feel the evil of the sisters penetrating him by his simply touching it.

Fancy.

He held it to his chest for a moment, not wanting to look at himself, wondering if this was folly. He was letting the sisters get to him. He had promised himself he wouldn't surrender to fears and superstitions. Yet he found himself wanting to look into the mirror. And he was worried about what he might see.

"Enough of this foolishness!" He gathered his courage, lifted the mirror and looked into it unflinchingly, determined to face his fears. At first glance he didn't seem much changed. His heart felt lighter and he indeed felt foolish for letting the sisters' threats invade his thoughts.

"Look closer, Prince." He dropped the mirror and was afraid he had broken it. Though it might have been a blessing if he had. He was sure it was Lucinda's voice he'd heard taunting him from the black ether, or wherever she deigned to dwell. It was Hell itself for all he knew. Picking up the mirror with a shaking hand, he took a second look. This time he did see deep lines round his eyes.

Gaston was right: he looked a good five years older after just a few months! The lines made his face look cruel. Heartless. All the things Circe had said he was.

Impossible.

His heart started to pound like thunder. It was pounding so violently that he felt as if it would burst within his chest.

Then came the laughter. It surrounded him, cacophonous. The wicked cackling seemed to come from lands unseen; their voices, their vindictive words entrapped him, causing his anxieties to overwhelm him. His vision became narrowed, and soon all he saw were the cat's yellow eyes staring at him from the mantel. Then everything closed in on him and his world became black.

Nothingness.

He was alone in the darkness with only the sisters' laughter and his own dread to keep him company.

He woke what seemed like days later, feeling as if he'd been beaten by a gang of villainous brutes.

His entire body ached and he could barely move. The sisters had ensured his misery and compounded it with their laughter and taunting, leaving him ill and suffering.

"You're awake, sir!" said Cogsworth from the corner chair, where he had been sitting. "We were very worried about you, sir."

"What happened?" The Prince's head was still befogged and he couldn't quite get his bearings.

"Well, it seems, sir, you were very ill, suffering from a severe fever. When you hadn't come down to breakfast, I came up to find you lying on the floor."

"Where's the mirror?"

"The mirror, sir? Oh yes, I put it away in your dressing stand."

The Prince's panic subsided. "Was it all a dream, then? All fancy brought on by worry or illness?"

"I don't know what you mean, sir. But you were rather ill. We're all very much relieved to hear you are out of the woods, as they say."

Cogsworth was putting on a brave face, as he always did, but the Prince could tell he had been worried. He looked tired, worn and uncustomarily rumpled. He was usually fastidious. It was a credit to his loyalty that it seemed he had been at the Prince's side during his entire illness.

"Thank you, Cogsworth. You're a good man."

"Thank you, sir. It was nothing."

Before Cogsworth could be embarrassed any further, the porter sheepishly poked his head into the room to say, "Excuse me, sir, Mrs Potts wants Cogsworth down in the kitchens."

"Here now, I won't have Mrs Potts telling me where I am needed!" grumbled Cogsworth.

"No, she's right, you look like you could use a good cup of tea," said the Prince. "I'm fine. Go to the kitchens before she waddles her way up here, getting angrier with each flight of stairs she has to take to reach us."

Cogsworth laughed at the thought of it. "Perhaps you're right, sir." He left the room, taking the porter along with him.

The Prince felt incredibly foolish for thinking he had actually been cursed. As he looked out of the window, the trees were violently swaying, dancing to a manic song only they were privy to. He longed to be outdoors, tracking elk and talking with his friend about anything other than the sisters, Circe or curses – and as if by magic, there was a knock at the door. It was Gaston.

"My friend! I heard you were awake! That Cogsworth wouldn't let anyone in your room except Dr Hillsworth, who just came downstairs to let us know you were finally on your way to health."

"Yes, Gaston, I'm feeling much better, thank you." Looking at Gaston, the Prince noticed he hadn't shaven in more than a few days, and the Prince wondered how long he had been ill.

"Have you been here all along, good friend?"

"I have. Cogsworth gave me a room in the East Wing, but I spent most of my time down in the kitchens with Mrs Potts and the others." Gaston seemed almost like the young boy the Prince had befriended so many years earlier, his face tensed with worry over his friend's illness – and spending his time in the kitchen like the other servants' children.

"Stay as long as you like. This was once your home, friend, and I want you to always feel it is such." Gaston looked touched by the sentiment but didn't say so.

"I'm going to make myself presentable before heading home. I'm sure things have gone to the winds without me there for so many days."

"Surely LeFou has it handled." The Prince tried not to look disappointed his friend was making plans to leave.

"Doubtful. He's a fool at best! Don't fret, my friend. I'm sure Cogsworth will be up shortly to keep you company and help you to make plans for the party we're throwing the moment you're well enough."

"Party?" the Prince asked.

Gaston gave one of his magic smiles, the kind that always ensured he would get his way. "Yes, a party, my friend, one that will be remembered throughout the ages!"

CHAPTER VI

GASTON'S GRAND IDEA

Gaston's plan was put into action only a few short weeks after the Prince's recovery. The entire staff was behind it and thought it was exactly what he needed.

"This is like a dream!" was heard throughout the castle by Mrs Potts as she amended menus and made suggestions for little cakes to be served in the great hall.

Cogsworth had an extra bounce in his step but was too austere to let it be known he was pleased to have a bustling house again to take control of like a general at war. And that was how he directed things, ordering the staff hither and thither to ready the castle for the grand event.

The Prince, however, had needed some persuading before he agreed to such a party. Gaston argued that after the mishap with Circe and his long illness, the Prince deserved a thrilling diversion.

"What better way to find the most enchanting woman in the kingdom than to invite every fair and available maiden so you may have your pick? And all under the guise of a fanciful ball?"

The Prince didn't share Gaston's enthusiasm.

"I hate such events, Gaston. I see no need to stuff my house with frilly ladies prancing around like decorated birds."

Gaston laughed.

"If we invite every fair maiden in the kingdom, Gaston, I daresay every single girl will attend!" the Prince protested.

"That is my point entirely, my friend! No girl would pass up her opportunity to shine in the Prince's eyes."

"But that is what I fear! Surely there will be far more ghastly-looking girls than beautiful! How shall I stand it?"

Gaston put his hand on his friend's shoulder and replied, "No doubt you will have to wade through some ugly ducklings before you find your princess, but won't it be worth it? What of your friend who had such a ball? Wasn't it a great success after the matter of the glass slipper was sorted?"

The Prince laughed. "Indeed, but you won't catch me marrying a housemaid like my dear friend, no matter how beautiful she is! Not after the disaster with the pig keeper."

The talk went on like that for many days, until the Prince decided he would have the ball after all, and why not? Why shouldn't he demand the attendance of every available maiden in the kingdom? He and Gaston would make a game of it, and if he did happen to find the young woman of his dreams, then all the better. So it was decided. He didn't have to think any more about it until the night of the event.

In the meantime he did his best to dodge his servants, who were running about like wild geese being chased by hounds. He forgave their

franticness and even grew to laugh when he heard
Mrs Potts padding her way down the hall to ask him
this or that about what he'd like served. Meanwhile,
the maids were polishing silver in the dining
room, the grooms were readying the stables for the
guests' horses and the parlour maids were perched
precariously on tall ladders, dusting the chandeliers
and replacing the old candles with new. The house
was abustle and he wanted nothing more than to
get outdoors and do some hunting. But Gaston was
out traversing his lands, dealing with one thing or
another, and couldn't be bothered with trivial sport.

The Prince chimed the bell for Cogsworth.

"Yes, sir, you rang?" asked Cogsworth, knowing
full well he had. The Prince always detested all
this ceremony, but he let Cogsworth have his way.
He remembered what his father – rest his soul –
had said to him many years ago. He said everyone
in the house, upstairs and down, had their places
and their roles to play. To deny a man like
Cogsworth his duty and remove him from his place
was like taking away his sense of self and dignity.

Cogsworth had treated him well for many years; he couldn't shatter the man's self-worth by treating him like family, even though that was how he had grown to think of him. It was an unspoken sentiment between them.

The Prince believed Cogsworth thought the same of him but was too austere to say so.

"Yes, Cogsworth, I would like you to arrange for the Maestro as soon as manageable. I mean to have another portrait."

Cogsworth rarely let his expression betray him. "Yes, sir, I shall send for him."

"What is it, Cogsworth? Don't you approve?"

It seemed he thought about it for a moment before answering. "It isn't my place to say so, sir, but if it was, I would mention how 'interesting' the household becomes when he visits."

The Prince had to laugh. He had thought Cogsworth was going to comment on how recently he'd had a portrait done.

"Indeed. He is a bit of a character, isn't he? He treats the staff well, though, doesn't he?"

"Oh no, sir, it isn't that. A gentleman such as the Maestro isn't the least bit challenging in that regard. No, sir, he's just an eccentric fellow, wouldn't you agree?"

"Yes he is, and very keen on himself and the impact his art makes on the world, I would say. Enough of that. I am sure you are very busy with all the details for tomorrow's event. I trust everything is in hand?"

Cogsworth looked positively proud, almost beaming. "Oh yes, everything is running like clockwork, sir. It's going to be a perfect evening."

"And Gaston, have you any word from him? He all but insisted I have this party and then took off to places unknown, leaving me here to dawdle my time away."

Cogsworth smirked. "Yes, sir, he sent word this morning assuring he would be back tomorrow morning. In the meantime, I've asked the gamekeeper to get ready for a day of stalking. I thought with the house in such a state you'd be eager to get outside."

"Brilliant idea, Cogsworth! Thank you!"

On the following evening the castle was aglow with gold flickering light, which was dancing in the hedge maze, making the animal topiaries seem to come to life. Everyone would be arriving within the hour, but the Prince was finding a moment of quiet in one of his favourite places on the castle grounds.

The tranquillity was shattered by Gaston's booming voice calling for him from the arched entryway covered in tiny pink blossoming roses.

"Are you in this damnable maze again, Prince?"

The Prince didn't answer his friend. He just sat there wondering what the night would bring. He had also been thinking of Circe and wondering if it was possible to ever find another girl who would love him as much as she had. There had been times he thought Circe was a dream and her sisters some sort of nightmare he had conjured in his own fevered imagination. He'd lost so much time already; it didn't seem reasonable to waste much more with thoughts of Circe, her harpy sisters or curses.

"Your guests will be arriving any moment," Gaston shouted, "and though he wouldn't admit it,

I think Cogsworth will blow a gasket if you're not there to greet them as they enter the great hall!"

The Prince sighed. "I'll be right there."

Gaston turned the corner, seeing his friend sitting near a towering topiary of a winged lion. "What's the matter? I thought this would liven your spirits! Every girl in three kingdoms is said to be attending! It's going to be magnificent!"

The Prince stood, straightening his velvet frock coat, and said, "Yes, it will be. Let's not keep the girls waiting."

The girls filed in by the hundreds. He didn't know there could be so many girls in all the world. All of them were decked out for the occasion. There were stunning brunettes with dark haunting eyes, pale and lovely blondes with perfect ringlets, striking redheads with jade-coloured eyes, and everything in between. They all paraded past him, some hiding behind their fans and giggling, while others tried not to look the least bit interested in whether he glanced in their direction. Some seemed too nervous to keep from trembling, sometimes so violently they lost their composure altogether and spilled their drinks.

There was one girl with auburn hair he didn't manage to see properly. She seemed to always have her back turned. She must have been very beautiful, because he caught the dirty glances she received from the other ladies as they passed her, and quite unlike the others, she didn't travel in a swarm of girls. She stood off alone – apart from almost everyone – seeming not the least bit interested in the idle chatter of the fairer sex.

"Gaston, who is that girl? The one in the blue dress I saw you talking with earlier? What's her name?" Gaston pretended he didn't recall, annoying the Prince. "You know very well to whom I'm referring, man! Now bring her over here and introduce me."

"You wouldn't be interested in her, trust me!"

The Prince raised an eyebrow.

"Wouldn't I? And why is that, my good friend?"

Gaston lowered his voice so those nearby wouldn't hear. "She's the daughter of Cuckoo!

Oh, she's lovely, yes, but her father is the laughing stock of the village! He's harmless enough, but fancies himself a great inventor! He's always building contraptions that clank, rattle and explode! She isn't the sort you'd like to get mixed up with, good friend."

"Perhaps you're right, but nevertheless, I would like to meet her."

"I daresay you would find her very tedious indeed with her endless talk of literature, fairy tales and poetry."

"You seem to know quite a bit about this girl, Gaston," the Prince said with a comical, knowing nod.

"I fear I do! In the few moments we spoke just now, she prattled on of nothing else. No, dear friend, we need to find you a *proper* lady. A princess! Someone like the Princess Morningstar over there. Now, she is a delight! No talk of books from her! I bet she's never read even a single book or had a thought of her own!"

The Prince thought that was a very good quality in a woman. He could do enough thinking for both himself and his future wife.

"Yes, bring over the Princess Morningstar. I'd very much like to meet her."

Princess Tulip Morningstar had long golden locks, with a milk-and-honey complexion and light sky-blue eyes. She looked like a doll draped in diamonds and pink silks.

She was remarkably beautiful – radiant, in fact. Everything about her sparkled, with one exception: her personality. But that didn't bother the Prince. Having an attractive personality was his job, not hers. It wouldn't do to have a wife who took attention away from him.

Princess Morningstar had a charming habit of giggling when she didn't have anything to contribute on a subject, which was most of the time. This made the Prince feel like the best of tutors. Honestly, he could talk about anything and her attentions were never diverted from him; she just giggled.

He'd already decided he was going to marry her, and judging by the sulky looks on the faces of the rest of the ladies in attendance, it must have been quite clear.

Gaston looked positively pleased with himself that he had helped arrange a perfect match for his friend. And for his part, he saw to it that the other ladies didn't go without a dance partner for very long.

It seemed to the Prince that Gaston must have danced with every girl there that evening – all except the inventor's daughter, who by all accounts didn't seem too pleased to be there to begin with, though he couldn't tell by the look on her face, because he hadn't, in fact, had a single clear glance at her the entire evening.

None of that mattered, though. He had his darling princess Tulip to look after now.

CHAPTER VII

THE PRINCESS AND THE PORTRAIT

The Prince was more pleased than ever the Maestro was coming to do his portrait now that he'd made Princess Tulip Morningstar his fiancée. It would be an engagement portrait with the two most attractive members of royalty anyone had beheld!

The princess went back to her father's kingdom after the ball and awaited the various ceremonies, parties and other trappings that would take place during their engagement, all leading up to, of course, the most majestic of weddings. She would, by custom, live with her family, visiting the Prince frequently with her nanny as chaperone, and sometimes also bringing her mother along as it suited her.

This time she would come with her nanny. Everyone was excited that the Prince had commissioned the Maestro to paint the portrait. He was the most celebrated painter in many kingdoms and was in great demand. Not since the renowned Master Maker of Mirrors had there been another artist who caused such a stir in the royal circles. Though his art could be brutally accurate, most gentry didn't seem to let that colour their opinion of the man.

Princess Tulip showed up on a rainy afternoon, quite soggy. Though her hair was flat and her clothes were sticking to her, she somehow managed to look pretty, and quite worth rescuing from the elements. The Prince kissed her sweetly on the cheek and greeted her happily when she stepped out of the carriage.

"Tulip, my love! How was your journey?"

A grumble came from inside the carriage, and out popped what must have been the young princess's nanny.

"It was intolerable, as you can see! The carriage leaked and I would be surprised if my darling girl doesn't come down with the nastiest of colds! I must get her into a hot bath at once!"

The Prince blinked a couple of times and smiled at the woman. She was impossibly old and lined like a little apple doll that had been mouldering away on a windowsill. Her hair and skin were powdery white, and though much aged, her eyes were rather sparkling with life. This woman was a little firecracker.

"I am so pleased to meet you at last, Nanny," he said as she wrinkled her nose at him as if there were a foul smell about the air.

"Yes, yes, very pleased to meet you, Prince, I'm sure. But won't you please show us to our rooms so I can get this girl into a hot bath?"

Cogsworth took things in hand. "If you will follow me, Princess, I will show you to your quarters so you may freshen yourself after your long journey."

And with that he took the ladies up the stairs and out of sight.

Well, the Prince thought, *this visit will be interesting with Nanny grumbling about.* Perhaps he could get Mrs Potts to divert her in the kitchens so he could have some time alone with his princess. He couldn't imagine what the week would be like with her around. His dread was squashed with the announcement of his other guest.

The Maestro!

He came promenading in with the dandiest of outfits – all velvet and lace in various shades of lilacs and blackberry. He had large sad eyes set into a slightly swollen face but seemed all the more handsome for it.

The Maestro looked as if he had a saucy story to share, and the Prince wondered if it would be unwise to seat Nanny and the Maestro at the same table that evening for dinner. His head spun at the thought of Nanny listening to the painter's outlandish stories. What he needed was Cogsworth. He would sort it all out.

And sort it out he did. Nanny dined with Mrs Potts, Cogsworth and the other staff downstairs at Mrs Potts's invitation. It wasn't custom by any means for a guest to eat with the downstairs staff, but Mrs Potts had a way with people, and by the end of the conversation, the two were swapping stories about the Prince and princess when they were young, determining which of them had been more insolent.

Meanwhile, dinner upstairs was delightfully charming. The servants had decorated the dining room splendidly. Rather than a large floral centrepiece, there were a number of smaller arrangements artfully placed on the table, evoking the feel of a garden infused with candlelight. There were many crystal bowls with floating flowers and candles, and the particular cut of crystal made an interesting use of the light, causing a fanciful effect of reflection on the walls and diners. It was quite beautiful. But not as beautiful as his darling love, the Prince thought.

The Maestro broke the silence. "To love in all its tantalizing and vexing forms!"

Tulip laughed behind her fan while the Maestro stood theatrically erect with his glass raised high in the air, waiting, it seemed, for someone to respond to his toast. The Prince feared the Maestro might stay there forever frozen in time like one of his paintings if he didn't say something quickly.

"Yes! To love," he agreed, and quickly added, "and to you, Maestro!"

Princess Tulip giggled again, warming the Prince's heart even more. He loved how sweet and demure she was, so content to sit idly, and always looking ravishing while doing so. He really couldn't have chosen a better maiden to be his bride.

"I couldn't be more pleased to have you, Maestro! I know you will capture the moment perfectly! We will look back on our engagement not only with fond memories but with – how was it you put it? Oh yes, our senses will instantly be assaulted with a profound and visceral recollection of that exact moment in time."

The Maestro looked pleased. "I'm honoured you remembered my words so vividly!" He then turned his attentions to the young lady, hoping to bring out something of her personality. "You must be brimming with utter excitement, Princess, are you not?"

The princess's eyes widened with wonder. She hardly knew what to say. "Oh yes, I am. I am very much looking forward to the wedding."

"Of course you are! But I was of course speaking of our painting! I will want to see an assortment of outfits from each of you for my approval, and we will need to discuss the topic of location. The rose garden seems like an enchanting setting, I would think! Yes, the rose garden it shall be! I have decided and there is no changing my mind!" He continued. "It seems every portrait that is painted with any real feeling is a portrait of the artist, and not of the sitter. I daresay you will both be magnificent!"

Tulip blinked more than a few times, trying to understand his meaning.

"Will you be in the portrait with us, Maestro?" she asked. Both gentlemen laughed.

Tulip didn't know if they were laughing at what she had said because it was clever or dull-witted, but she decided to act as though it had been the cleverest thing she could possibly have said, and hoped the topic would change to something she needn't partake in.

The Maestro, seeing the dread in her face, added, "Don't fret, dear Tulip. I am so clever that sometimes I don't understand a single word of what I am saying."

To this the princess could reply only by saying, "Oh!" and then giggling some more, which seemed to please everyone, because they joined in her laughter.

The next morning the magnificent trio was found in the rose garden as the Maestro sketched and the lovers did their best to hold their poses without giving the master painter cause to become cross with them.

"Prince, please! This is supposed to be the happiest moment of your life and your face looks like you've been eating something sour! Why do you look so displeased? What could you possibly be thinking of that causes one's face to contort so?"

The Prince had in fact been thinking about the last time he was in the rose garden, the night he had parted with Circe. The events had become blurred in his mind and he was trying hard to make sense of it all. Surely Circe had brought along her wicked sisters and they had proclaimed he was cursed for his misdeeds. He was certain he hadn't imagined it, but the curse itself, that was balderdash ... wasn't it? Sometimes he couldn't help fearing it might be true.

The Prince was brought out of his thoughts by Cogsworth's voice.

"Lunch is served."

The Maestro slammed down his drawing coals, cracking them into tiny powdery bits. "Very well! I think I prefer to lunch in my room! Alone!" he huffed, and he stormed away, not uttering a single word of salutation to either of the happy couple. Rather than giggling, as we well know was Tulip's way, she wilted into a heap of tears at being scolded.

The Prince, it seemed, had his hands entirely full with the fitful Maestro, his weeping Tulip and her sour nanny. How would the rest of the week go?

CHAPTER VIII

THE WILTING FLOWER

The next day Princess Tulip Morningstar and the Prince shared a very quiet breakfast together in the morning room. She didn't ask the Prince where he had been the night before, or why he had missed dinner. She had been forced to dine with the Maestro by herself and was mortified when he enquired where the Prince might have been and she couldn't answer. She wanted to rail on him, honestly. Inwardly she was seething, but Nanny warned her never to let her anger show. It wasn't ladylike to appear upset. Nanny said that far too often a woman unknowingly sabotaged herself when reproaching her husband for his misdeeds. To stay quiet and say nothing was reproach itself. But to say something only gave him reason to turn the situation on to the lady, claiming that she was overly emotional and making more of the situation than needed, causing him to become angry with her.

Tulip didn't understand this entirely, but she did notice that Nanny didn't follow her own advice, and thought perhaps that was why Nanny had never married. So she said nothing. The only sounds in the room were those of the dishes clanking and the birds singing outside the lovely morning-room windows. The room was made entirely of paned windows and had the most breathtaking view of the garden. Tulip thought of herself in the future, sitting here looking out of these windows by the hour, languishing. She wished the Prince would say something, anything to break this silence. She couldn't think of what to say; anything she said would surely sound reproachful, and her tone – she wasn't at all positive it could be tempered.

So Tulip just sat there drinking her tea and picking at her scone, waiting for the Prince to speak.

And while waiting, she thought about that girl she'd met at the ball. Oh, what was her name? It was pretty, rather musical. She was probably the sort of girl who would rebuke the Prince in a situation like this – demand, in fact, to know where the Prince had been the night before. Then again, the girl with the pretty name was probably not the sort of girl a prince would want to marry. She sighed. Her thoughts were halted with the sound of his voice at last.

"Tulip."

Her eyes brightened when she heard him say her name.

"Yes?" she responded, hoping he would at last make his amends for stealing away the previous night and leaving her alone to listen to the Maestro talk endlessly about his art.

"We'd better not keep the Maestro waiting."

Her heart sank.

"Of course, shall we go to the rose garden?"

"Yes, I suppose we should."

The rest of the week went on very much the same. Princess Tulip Morningstar pouted and played with the castle's cat, the Maestro gesticulated wildly while making grand speeches about art at every opportunity, and the Prince escaped every evening to the tavern with Gaston the moment they were done sitting for the Maestro.

On the day of the unveiling of the new portrait, quite a little family party had been arranged. Tulip was in better spirits to have her mother, Queen Morningstar, there, as well as some of her ladies to attend her. Also present was Gaston, as well as a few other close friends of the Prince's. King Morningstar of course couldn't take time away from his duties at court but sent along lavish gifts for both his daughter and his future son-in-law.

After they had feasted well on what was one of Mrs Potts's most outstanding dinners to date, everyone went into the great hall to partake in the unveiling of the portrait. The great hall was filled with paintings of the Prince's entire family, including portraits of him that had been painted from the time he was a wee lad.

"Ah! I see you've hung the Maestro's portrait here in the great hall, where it belongs. Good choice, old man!" said Gaston as he looked upon faces he had grown up with.

"Yes, I thought it was better suited in here."

A rather loud clearing of the throat was heard from the other side of the room, where the Maestro was standing. It seemed he thought the occasion required more ceremony and this idle chat was debasing the situation at hand. Thank goodness he wouldn't have to suffer this company much longer.

"Yes, well, without further delay, I would like to share the latest of my greatest treasures." With that, the faithful servant Lumiere pulled the cord, which dropped the black silk cloth that had been concealing the painting. The room erupted into a loud clatter of sighs and applause. Everyone seemed to be highly impressed with the painting, and the Maestro soaked in the praise that was being heaped upon him like an actor on the stage would – bowing at the waist and placing his hand upon his heart to indicate that he was very touched indeed.

No doubt he actually was.

The Prince couldn't help noticing how harshly he had been painted in the portrait. His eyes looked cruel, piercing, almost like those of a wolf seeking his prey, and his mouth looked thinner, more sinister than it had looked before. Gaston knocked the Prince with his elbow.

"Say something, man! They're expecting a speech!" he whispered in the Prince's ear.

"I couldn't have asked for a more beautiful portrait of my lovely bride-to-be!" the Prince finally uttered.

Princess Tulip blushed deeply and said, "Thank you, my love. And I, too, couldn't have asked for a more handsome and dignified visage of my prospective husband."

Dignified? Wasn't that a word one used for older men? Did he look *dignified?* His visage, as she called it, looked harsh and worn, not one of a man who had not yet reached his 20th birthday, but one of a man well into his 40s. This simply wouldn't do. *Dignified!*

The party was led out of the great hall and into the music room, where a group of musicians waited to entertain them. By all accounts the evening went on pleasantly enough, but the Prince couldn't take his mind off the painting. He looked so worn, so ugly. Had Tulip agreed to marry him simply because she would eventually be queen in these lands? Did she love him at all?

He couldn't see how.

He slipped away from the party to confirm the Maestro's rendition of him in his bedroom mirror. He just stood there staring, trying to find himself in the man staring back at him. Why hadn't anyone said anything? How could he have changed so much in so little time?

Later that evening, when the Prince's guests and staff were all tucked into their beds, the Prince stole out of his rooms and made his way down the long, dark corridor. He was fearful of waking Queen Morningstar. She would of course think he was sneaking into the princess's chamber, but that was the farthest thing from his mind now.

When he passed Tulip's room, a creaking sound startled him, but it was only that blasted cat pushing the door open. He had no idea why the princess liked it so much. There was something sinister about the way the feline looked at him, and something eerie in her markings, which made her look like a creature that roamed cemeteries rather than castle grounds.

Well, if the queen did wake to find him prowling the halls, she wouldn't believe he was on his way to look at his painting again. He'd been sleeping fitfully and unable to rest, his thoughts consumed by that ghastly painting. Once he got into the great hall and managed to light the candles, he stood there staring at the painting again. He had indeed changed – that had been clear when he looked at himself in the mirror earlier that evening – but surely the Maestro had dramatized the changes. Just look at the difference between this painting and the last, which had been done less than a year earlier. There was no way a man could change so dramatically. He would never forgive the Maestro for creating the unfavourable rendering. He decided the man must pay for such an uncharitable act.

The beautiful orange-and-black cat seemed to be in accord with the Prince, because she narrowed her eyes in much the same way he did when he plotted his revenge.

At the Prince's encouragement, Cogsworth had all visiting guests packed and stuffed into the carriages very early the next morning. Mrs Potts was disappointed not to have the opportunity to serve the guests breakfast before the start of their travels, so she packed a large trunk with lovely things for them to eat on their journey. The sun was barely visible, and the tops of the trees were obscured in mist. There was a terrible chill in the air, so it didn't seem unreasonable that the Prince was eager to get back indoors, where he could warm himself.

He made his goodbyes to his guests, thanking them all and bidding them farewell, with promises of love and letter-writing to Tulip. He sighed with great relief when the carriages drove away.

Gaston, who had been standing silently at his side, finally spoke.

"So why was it you woke me at this ungodly hour, my friend?"

"I need a little favour. Some time back you mentioned a particularly unscrupulous fellow who can be called upon for certain deeds."

Gaston raised his eyebrows. "Surely there are ways to get out of marrying the princess other than having her killed!"

The Prince laughed.

"No, man! I mean the Maestro! I would like you to make the arrangements for me. The incident cannot be traced back to me, you understand?"

Gaston looked at his friend and said, "Absolutely!"

"Thank you, good friend. And once that is sorted, what do you say to a day of hunting?"

"Sounds perfect! I would like nothing more."

CHAPTER IX

THE STATUE IN THE OBSERVATORY

As Princess Tulip Morningstar's carriage rolled up the path leading to the Prince's castle, she thought there was nothing more breathtaking than the sight of the castle in wintertime. Her father's kingdom was beautiful, yes, but it didn't compare to the Prince's, especially when it was covered in white snow and decorated for the winter solstice.

The entire castle was infused with light and glowing brightly in the dark winter night. She had high hopes for this visit and wished nothing more than for the Prince to treat her with kindness and love like he once had. Surely the winter holiday would cheer his sour mood of late and bring him back around to the man she'd fallen in love with that dreamy night at the ball.

"Look, Nanny, isn't it beautiful the way the pathway is lined with candlelight?"

Nanny smiled. "Yes, my dear child, it's very beautiful. Even more lovely than I imagined."

Tulip sighed.

"What is it, Tulip? What's troubling you?"

Tulip said nothing. She loved her nanny dearly and couldn't bring herself to ask her what she'd been rehearsing the entire way from her father's kingdom to their destination.

"I think I know, dear heart, and don't you fret. I won't give the Prince any reason to be upset this visit, I promise you. Nanny will keep her thoughts to herself this time."

Tulip smiled and kissed her nanny on her soft powdery cheek.

"That's right, give your old nanny a kiss and forget your troubles. It's solstice, dear, your favourite time of year, and nothing will ruin this for you, I promise you that!"

The carriage reached the front doors of the castle, where Lumiere was standing, waiting to open her carriage door.

"*Bonjour*, Princess! Aren't you looking as beautiful as always? It is so lovely to see you again!"

Tulip giggled and blushed, as she often did when Lumiere spoke to her.

"Hello, Lumiere. I trust the Prince is attending to more pressing matters than taking time to greet his fiancée, who has travelled across the country to visit him for the solstice?" grumbled Nanny.

Lumiere took it in stride. "Indeed, Nanny! If both of you will follow me, Christian will take your luggage to your apartments in the East Wing."

Nanny and Tulip looked at each other in wonder. Usually they would be shown up to their rooms so they might refresh themselves after their long travels. But Lumiere ushered them past many vast and beautiful rooms until they finally arrived at a large door wrapped to look like an extravagant gift with a big gold bow.

"What is this?" Nanny snapped.

"Go inside and see for yourself!"

Tulip opened the giant gift-wrapped door to find a winter wonderland within. There was an enormous oak tree stretching to the very height of the golden domed ceiling. It was covered in magnificent lights and beautifully ornate finery that sparkled in their glow. Under the tree was an abundance of gifts, and standing among them was the Prince, his arms stretched out as he waited to greet her. Tulip's heart was filled with joy. The Prince seemed to be in wonderful spirits!

"My love! I am so happy to see you!" She wrapped her arms round his waist and embraced him.

"Hello, my dearest. You are in quite a state from travelling, aren't you? I'm surprised you didn't insist to be taken to your rooms to make yourself presentable before showing yourself."

The Prince scowled as if he were looking at a dirty servant girl and not the woman he loved.

"I'm sorry, dear, you're right, of course."

Lumiere, always the gentleman, and eager to please the ladies, added, "It's my fault, my lord.

I insisted she follow me at once. I knew you were excited to show the princess the decorations."

"I see. Well, Tulip dear, soon you will be queen in these lands and, more importantly, queen in this house, and you must learn to decide for yourself what is right and insist upon it. I am sure next time you will make the right choice."

Tulip coloured a deep crimson but found the most authoritative voice she could manage.

"Yes, my love and prince. Lumiere, if you will show Nanny and me to our rooms so we may ready ourselves for dinner...."

With that, she left the room without even a kiss for the Prince, for she was rushing to avoid letting him see she was on the verge of tears.

How dare he suggest she was too unseemly to come into his company upon her arrival? Did she look so grotesque? Lumiere seemed to hear her very thoughts.

"As I said when you arrived, dear princess," he said, "you look beautiful, as always. Do not heed the master's words. He has been rather distracted of late."

The Beast Within

Nanny and Tulip just looked at each other, wondering what this visit had in store.

CHAPTER X

THE OBSERVER IN THE OBSERVATORY

It seemed to Tulip there were fewer servants than the last time she visited, though the castle didn't seem to suffer for it; it looked even more grand than usual, having been decorated for the solstice. Her favourite court companion, Pflanze, a beautiful black, orange and white cat, was in attendance to keep her company. "Hello, beautiful Pflanze!" she said to her little friend, and she leaned over to pat her on the head.

"So you've named her? What a strange name. What does it mean?"

Tulip looked up to see the Prince standing over her.

"Oh! I don't know! I thought you came up with it. I was sure it was you who told me her name," the princess responded.

"It wasn't me. I don't even like the beast!" he said, giving Pflanze a dirty look as she gave him her customary side glance and adjusted her paws.

"Someone else must have told me," said Tulip.

"Indeed! That is clear, someone else would have had to tell you! I could puzzle that out on my own! And like the featherhead you are apt to be, you've completely forgotten who told you. But clearly someone else told you!"

"Yes," said Tulip in the tiniest of voices, trying desperately not to let her lip quiver as he went on.

"Never mind! I see you've not changed for dinner yet! Well, we can't keep Mrs Potts waiting. What you're wearing will just have to do! Come! I'll escort you into the dining room, even if you're not fit for the grand affair planned in your honour."

Tulip's heart sank and her face turned scarlet. She had, in fact, changed for dinner and made herself up considerably well – at least, she thought she had. She was wearing one of her finest gowns and had thought she looked quite beautiful before she started down the stairway. She made a special effort to look flawless in light of what had happened upon her arrival. Now she wanted nothing more than to run away from this place and never come back again, but she was trapped. Trapped with this terrible prince! She didn't care how rich he was, or how massive his kingdom or influence; she couldn't stand the idea of being married to such a bully. How would she get out of it? She didn't know what to do. She decided to stay quiet on the matter until she could talk to Nanny.

After dinner Tulip asked the Prince if he'd like to go on a walk, and he agreed. He was being sullen and quiet but not cross, so for that, at least, she was thankful. They walked around the lake, which was frozen at this time of year but still breathtakingly beautiful.

"Could you show me the observatory, sweetheart? The sky is very clear and I should like to see the view you've spoken of so frequently."

"If you'd like."

They climbed the long stone spiral staircase until they reached the top floor of the observatory. Even without the telescope, the view was spellbinding. Tulip could see the entire sky through the glass domed ceiling. She felt as if the stars were winking back at her for how joyfully she looked upon them.

It seemed they were not the only ones who had decided it was a good night to stargaze. Someone was already looking through the telescope when they reached the top of the stairs.

"Hello! Who's there?"

The observer didn't answer.

"I said, who's there?"

Tulip was frightened, especially after the Prince motioned her to get behind him for protection – but as the Prince got closer to the intruder, he realized it wasn't a person at all, but a statue.

"What's this?" He was nonplussed. There had never been a statue up here before, and how on earth had someone got it up here without some sort of elaborate apparatus? There was no way something that heavy could have been brought up the stairs without his knowing.

Tulip started to giggle in nervous relief. "Oh my! It's just a statue! I feel silly for being so startled!"

But the Prince still had a look of confusion on his face while she prattled on.

"But it does look kind of creepy, doesn't it? It almost looked like it was giving us a side glance when we walked in! And how odd a pose for a statue, leaning over looking into the telescope! It obstructs our ability to look through it completely! I'm sure this wasn't your idea, dear! Honestly, I don't think I like it. I can't tell if it's meant to be a man or a woman. Male or female, though, it does look horrified, don't you think? Like something terrible came upon it and turned it into stone?"

The Prince hardly heard her rambling; his mind was suddenly violated by terrible disembodied voices from the past.

Your castle and its grounds shall also be cursed, then, and everyone within will be forced to share your burden.

Nothing but horrors will surround you, from when you look into a mirror to when you sit in your beloved rose garden.

The Prince shuddered at the sound of the witch's voice ringing in his ears. Was he cursed after all? First the drastic change in his appearance and now this strange event?

His servants trapped within stone? He couldn't imagine what it would be like to be trapped like that. He wondered if the trapped person could hear their conversation. If the person was aware he had been entrapped in stone. The thought sent shivers up the Prince's spine.

"Darling, you look peaky! What's the matter?" Princess Tulip asked.

The Prince's heart was racing, his chest felt heavy, and it was hard for him to breathe. He suddenly realized everything the sisters had said was coming true.

"Tulip! Do you love me? I mean, truly love me?"

When she looked at him, he looked like a lost little boy and not the spiteful bully he'd been to her as of late.

"I do, my love! Why do you ask?"

He grabbed her hand and held it tightly.

"But would you still love me if I were somehow disfigured?"

"What a question! Of course I would!"

Her heart was again softening to the Prince. Not since the night they had met and he had asked her to marry him had he been so kind.

"You know that I love you, my darling! I love you more than anything!" he said desperately as tears welled up in her eyes at his sweet words.

"I do now, my love! I do now!"

Princess Tulip Morningstar was happier than she had dared hope on Solstice Eve. She hadn't imagined such a turn of character in the Prince, but since that night in the observatory, he'd been nothing but sweet to her.

"Oh, Nanny! I do love him so!" she whispered while sipping her spiced wine.

"How quickly you pivot from one emotion to another, my dear!" said Nanny.

"But, Nanny! His disposition has fluctuated greatly from one moment to the next! But I do feel he's finally himself again."

Nanny did not look convinced.

"We shall see, my dear."

The Prince did look glad, Nanny had to admit, and he seemed to be falling all over himself to make Tulip happy. It was almost comical, actually, quite like a mockery of love. But her Tulip was happy, so she didn't press the matter or cast an evil eye in his direction. She did notice, however, Pflanze, who was perched on Tulip's lap, looking at the Prince with hateful eyes. Nanny had to wonder why that cat disliked him so. Perhaps she too saw through this ruse.

The Prince was very pleased with the Solstice Eve gathering. He was a bit exhausted by his attentions to Tulip, but he had decided there was no better way of breaking the curse than marrying Princess Morningstar. It was clear she loved him a great deal, so he was already half way there. All he had to do now was make the sisters believe that he loved her, too.

The Observer in the Observatory

Of course, there were indeed things about her that he loved. He loved her beauty, her coyness and how she kept her opinions to herself. There was nothing he hated more than a girl with too many opinions of her own.

He liked that she showed no interest in books, and that she didn't prattle on about her pastimes. In fact, he had no idea how she spent her time when she wasn't in his company. It was as if she didn't exist when she wasn't with him. He imagined her sitting in a little chair in her father's castle, waiting for him to send for her.

He loved how she never gave him a cross look or scorned him even when he was in the foulest of moods. He loved how easy she was to manage. Surely that counted for something; surely that was a form of love, was it not? And he figured the sweeter he was to her, the more quickly he would reverse the curse.

That was the aim of this visit, to show the sisters how much he loved Princess Tulip Morningstar. But how would he get their attention?

Oh yes, they had said the Prince and his beloved had to seal their love with a kiss. Well, that would be easy enough. He would just have to spirit her away to a romantic setting and *bam!* A kiss! A kiss she would never forget!

He arranged the entire thing with Lumiere, who was best at planning such romantic things.

'Romantic interludes' he called them. "Oh yes, Prince, she will melt into your arms in utter delight when she sees what we have in store for her, mark my words!"

"Wonderful, Lumiere. And Mrs Potts – she's sorted a hamper for the picnic, has she?"

"Everything is taken care of, even the nanny. We invited her to a tea party downstairs so she will be very well occupied and you lovebirds will be able to fly free without worry of her watchful gaze."

The Prince laughed. Lumiere was always so poetic when he spoke of love, so devoted to the notion of it. The Prince couldn't go wrong with having him arrange this little escapade, and he was sure Tulip would be very happy.

CHAPTER XI

MORNING TEA

The following day, in the morning room, Tulip was working at some needlepoint while idly petting Pflanze as the cat pawed at some spools of thread that fell on to her red velvet cushion.

Nanny was talking, presumably to Tulip, about Mrs Potts's crumble and wondering how hard it would be to wrangle the recipe out of her, when Lumiere entered the room.

"Excuse me, lovely ladies, but my dear Tulip, could you possibly spare your nanny for a few moments? Mrs Potts has arranged a little tea for Nanny downstairs. I think she is eager for your company, Nanny."

Nanny looked at Lumiere with a sly grin.

"And yes, Nanny, to be sure, she has baked a peach crumble for the tea. She knows how fond you are of her crumbles."

Nanny smiled. "Tulip, dear, you wouldn't mind, would you? You won't feel too lonely if Nanny slipped away for a spot of tea with old Mrs Potts?"

Tulip grinned at her nanny and said, "Of course not, Nanny, I have Pflanze to keep me company." And then, looking at Pflanze, she added, "Don't I, sweet girl?"

Pflanze just looked at Tulip with her large, black-rimmed golden eyes, tinted with tiny flakes of green, and blinked them slowly at her as if to say, "Yes."

"See! I will be fine! Go have your tea!"

And off Nanny went.

Tulip didn't know what she would do without Nanny. But she knew once she was married, she couldn't justify having her in the household. She would, of course, have a lady's servant – someone to do her hair, to help her dress, to arrange her jewels –

but it wouldn't be the same. She couldn't imagine sharing her feelings with anyone but Nanny. Perhaps since she and Mrs Potts had become so friendly, it wouldn't seem strange to keep Nanny on. She would have to talk to her mother about that when she returned from her trip. But what if her mother was unable to spare Nanny or thought it was somehow inappropriate for Tulip to bring her along? That was just too dreadful to think of now.

The Prince peeked into the room, taking Tulip's mind off her future household concerns. She knew he didn't like Pflanze sitting on his fine cushions, but she couldn't help indulging the creature, and he didn't seem to notice.

"Hello, my love. I have a little surprise for you. Do you think I can steal you away while we don't have Nanny to worry about? She's always snooping around and wondering where you are."

Tulip's face transformed into something shining and bright. She couldn't remember ever being so happy, not even when her father gave her Cupcake, her favourite horse. Oh, Cupcake! She couldn't wait to see her again. She wondered if the Prince would object to Cupcake's coming to live here once they were married. So many things to think about.

"Darling?" His voice brought Tulip out of her deep thoughts.

"Oh, yes, dear, I'm sorry. I was just thinking about how much I love you! And how sweet you are for asking Mrs Potts to invite Nanny for tea so we could have some time together alone."

The Prince smiled. His featherhead had puzzled out his ruse. What a surprise.

"So you worked out my clever scheme? Aren't you a cunning girl?" he said. "Come now! I have something I would like to show you."

"What is it?" Tulip squealed like an excited little girl.

"You will just have to wait and see, my love, but first you will have to put this on."

He handed her a long white piece of silk.

She looked at him queerly.

"It's a surprise, my love. Trust me." He helped her tie the blindfold and led her to what she was sure was the courtyard. He let go of her hand and gently kissed her on the cheek. "Count to 50, my dear, and then take off the blindfold."

He could see she was frightened.

"My dear, you're trembling. There's nothing to fear, I promise. I'll be waiting for you at the end of your journey."

"My ... *journey?*" Her voice sounded so small and confused.

"It won't be a long journey, my princess, and the way will be quite clear. Now count to 50."

She could hear his footfalls moving farther and farther away as she counted in her mind. It was silly to be so frightened, but she hated nothing more than the dark. Nanny had tried everything, but Tulip's relentless fear of darkness never diminished. She tried not to count too quickly so she wouldn't ruin the Prince's surprise, but found herself becoming too fearful of the confining darkness. "Forty-eight, forty-nine, fifty!" She ripped the silk sash from her eyes. It took a moment for them to adjust before she saw the path laid before her. The tips of her toes touched the scattered pink rose petals that had been strewn across the courtyard to create a path that led right into the hedge maze. Her fears fluttered away as she quickly walked upon the petals, eager to venture into the maze constructed of animal topiaries. The petals led her past an exceptionally large serpent, its mouth gaping wide and bearing long, deadly fangs. The serpent twisted its way round the corner, revealing a part of the maze she'd never seen. It was a replica of the castle, almost exact in every way, except without the many griffons and gargoyles perched on every corner and turret. She imagined her future children playing here one day, laughing and making a game of the animals in the maze. What a lovely place this would be for children. She stopped her daydreaming and followed the rose petals past several whimsical animals, some of which she didn't know. She often felt cheated having been born a girl, not having had tutors like her brother had or the freedom to explore the world. Women learned of the world through their fathers, their brothers and, if they were lucky, their husbands. It didn't seem quite fair.

She was accomplished for a girl – she knew how to sew, sing, paint watercolours and even play the harpsichord fairly well – but she could not name all the animals in what would soon be her own hedge maze. She felt stupid most of the time and hoped others didn't see her in that light but feared they usually did.

"Never mind that," she said to herself, and was surprised to see that the trail of petals led out of the hedge maze and away from the mysterious animals that made her feel foolish and into a lovely garden she hadn't yet seen on her visits here.

It was enclosed with a low semicircle wall, and within were lovely bright-coloured flowers. For a moment she thought she found herself stumbling upon springtide; it was such a remarkable sight, so bright and full of life in the middle of the wintry landscape. She couldn't fathom how the flowers thrived in such bitter cold. Scattered among the flowers were beautiful statues, characters from legends and myths; she knew that much from listening in on her brother's lessons with his tutors before Nanny would take her away to practise her walking.

Practise walking, indeed!

No wonder men didn't take women seriously; they had classes in walking while men learned ancient languages.

The garden was stunning, and very much like a fairy tale, filled with the cold blue light of the winter afternoon. Nestled in the centre of the enchanted garden, all pink and gold, was a stone bench, where her dearest was waiting for her, smiling with his hand outstretched.

"It's so beautiful, my love! How is this possible?"

The Prince's smile broadened.

"I arranged flowers from the hothouse to be moved here so you may experience the joy of spring."

She sighed.

"You're amazing, my dearest! Thank you," she said coyly as she lowered her eyes to the flowers in the snow.

The Prince decided this was the moment – the moment when he would kiss her and break the curse.

"May I kiss you, my love?"

Tulip looked around as if expecting her mother or Nanny to jump out from the hedge maze or pop out from behind a statue, and then, deciding she didn't care if they did, she kissed him! And then she kissed him again, and again.

As they walked back to the castle, the Prince seemed happier and more at ease than she'd ever known him to be. It was all so unexpected – this wonderful day, his attentiveness, everything that had happened on this visit, really. She felt much better about their upcoming marriage. She had been so terribly worried before, and now she could hardly recall why.

"Did you hear that, Tulip?" The Prince's mood shifted from gleeful to panicked.

"Hear what, dear?"

She hadn't heard a thing aside from the birds singing in the nearby snow-covered trees.

"That noise – it sounded like an animal, like a growl."

Tulip laughed, making a joke of it.

"Perhaps the hedge animals have come to life and they are going to eat us alive!"

The Prince looked as though he'd taken her jest quite seriously. His eyes were darting about as he tried to find the location of the wild beast.

"You don't really think there is an animal in here with us, do you?"

When she realized he was, in fact, serious, she became very frightened.

"I don't know, Tulip, stay right here. I'm going to check it out."

"No! Don't leave me here alone! I don't want to be eaten by whatever is prowling around in here!"

The Prince was becoming very impatient.

"You won't if you stay here like I've told you. Now be quiet and please do let go of my hand!"

He ripped his hand away from hers before she could comply with his request, and she stood there frozen in fear as the Prince dashed off looking for wild beasts.

She stayed there fretting for some time before he came back for her.

"Oh my goodness!" she gasped.

The Prince was badly clawed across his forearm. Whatever had attacked him had clawed right through his jacket and left deep, bloody wounds in his arm.

"My love, you're hurt!"

The Prince looked stricken and angry.

"Brilliant of you to have surmised that, my dear," he moaned.

"What happened? What attacked you?" she said, trying not to let his bad temper affect her.

"Clearly some sort of wild beast with huge, sharp claws."

She knew it was better to ask nothing more in case she provoked him into further bitterness.

"Let's get you back to the castle so we can have that taken care of."

They walked back in silence. She felt like his attitude towards her had completely shifted again. She tried to put it out of her mind, but she couldn't help feeling his anger was directed at her and not at the beast that had attacked him.

She wanted to cry, but she knew that would just make him angrier, so she walked back to the castle saying nothing, hoping his temper would improve.

CHAPTER XII

THE MYSTERY OF THE SERVANTS

Cogsworth did not greet them at the door as he normally did; instead it was Lumiere.

"Where is Cogsworth? I need him to fetch the doctor!" the Prince barked.

Lumiere looked worried, but not just for his master. It seemed as if something else was going on, something he dreaded telling the Prince.

"Of course, my lord. I shall take care of it."

As he was walking away to have one of the porters send a message for the doctor, the Prince said, "And send me Cogsworth!"

Lumiere stopped dead in his tracks and it took a few moments before he turned round to respond.

"Well, sir, you see, we don't know where Cogsworth is."

"What on earth are you talking about, you don't know where he is? He's always here! Go and find him at once and tell him I need him! Never mind! I will ring for him myself."

He went to the mantel to pull the cord that summoned Cogsworth.

"Excuse me, sir, but he's not there. We've searched the entire estate and we cannot find him. We're all very worried."

The Prince raged. He was going out of his mind with anger.

"This is nonsense! Where on earth is the man? It's not like him to shirk his duties!"

"I know, sir, that is why we are all so worried. Mrs Potts is in a heap of tears downstairs! She's had Chip looking everywhere for him. Everyone has been looking, sir. Do you recall the last time you saw him?"

He couldn't.

"Come to think of it, I have not seen him all day."

"This is all very vexing," Tulip interjected, "but I think we should call the doctor, don't you? I'm worried about your arm, my love."

Lumiere was rattled out of his panic for his friend Cogsworth and switched his focus to his master.

"Yes, of course, I'd better take care of that first thing, sir, and then we will arrange another search for Cogsworth."

CHAPTER XIII

THE BOUNDER

The entire household was in a panic. Cogsworth was nowhere to be found, and now it seemed Mrs Potts was also missing. "But, Nanny, it doesn't make sense! You were just having tea with her. Where in the world would she have gone off to?"

Nanny's eyes were red from crying.

"I don't know! I went to fetch us some more hot water for the tea. That Mrs Potts is always bustling about, and I just wanted her to sit for a spell. You know that woman can't just sit down to enjoy a nice cup of tea without getting this or that for one person or another. But wouldn't you know it, once I returned with the water, she was gone!

And the strangest thing, sitting there on the table was a pretty little teapot as round as can be!"

Tulip was confused.

"Nanny, you were having tea. I don't understand why a pot upon the table would be so strange."

Nanny said, "Ah, but you see, I had the teapot we were using, didn't I? To get the water. So why was there another just sitting on the table?"

"That is strange, I suppose."

Nanny's face crinkled up.

"It's much more than strange, girl! Something is happening in this house! Something sinister! I felt it the first time we arrived here and now it's getting stronger!"

Tulip wasn't going to let Nanny get her worked up with her superstitious nonsense. She'd done it far too often in the past, and she wouldn't allow herself to be swept away by it again. Not now.

"Oh, I know what you're thinking, girl! You think Nanny is an old, foolish woman, but I've been on this earth much longer than most and I've seen things most people only dream of."

Tulip rolled her eyes, but Nanny went on.

"I'm telling you, I think this place is cursed."

Both ladies looked up from their conversation when they heard Lumiere clearing his throat at the room's threshold.

"I just wanted you to know the doctor has left and the Prince is resting comfortably."

"Will he be okay?" Tulip asked, worried.

"Oh yes, he will be fine. He's recovering and exhausted, that's all. I'm sure he will want to see you tomorrow," he said, smiling in an attempt to lighten the mood.

Tomorrow? Not today? Tulip wondered, but she smiled back at Lumiere. She couldn't help it; there was something about him.

"You needn't fuss over us this evening for dinner, Lumiere," she said. "You can just bring us something on a tray. We can eat in our rooms or perhaps next to the fire in the sitting room. I'm sure everyone is in quite a tizzy down there with Mrs Potts and Cogsworth missing. I wouldn't want any of you worrying over us."

Nanny looked pleased with the job she had done raising Tulip; she sounded not only like a real queen but a very compassionate one at that. But the flirty little Frenchman wouldn't hear of serving guests on trays in the sitting room or any other room aside from the dining hall.

"Oh, no! That will not do! If Mrs Potts were here, she would blow her lid at the thought of you two eating off trays! And as for the menu this evening, never fear, we have something special planned for you!" He smiled another magical grin and said, "The dressing gong will be at six o'clock, dinner at eight o'clock. See you then!"

Then he was gone, most likely dashing his way downstairs to arrange dinner and supervise the search for the missing servants. Tulip looked at her nanny coyly. "You don't think the two of them sneaked off together? Cogsworth and Mrs Potts? You don't think they're in love?"

Nanny laughed. "I wish it were as simple as that, my girl, but no. Neither of them gave me the slightest notion there was something between them. No, I fear something dreadful has happened to them."

Tulip rolled her eyes again. "Stop with all the talk of curses, Nanny! I won't have it!"

Later that night, in the main dining hall, you wouldn't have known two of the most important people on the staff were missing. The room looked lovely, decorated with some of the hothouse flowers from Tulip's surprise earlier in the day, and the candles were sparkling brightly in crystal votive bowls, casting an unearthly light. The two ladies were enjoying their dessert when the Prince stumbled into the room looking half crazed.

"I'm happy you ladies are enjoying your meal while the entire household is falling into disarray around you!" He looked terribly worn, as though he'd aged several years from the ordeal. Nanny and Tulip just stared at him, at a complete loss.

"Have you nothing to say for yourself, Tulip? Sitting there stuffing yourself while my childhood companions are suffering such a terrible fate?"

Nanny spoke first.

"Here now! I won't have you speaking to her like that. She's been worried sick over them and you. We both have!"

His face turned into something inhuman, something wicked and cruel. Nanny feared the Prince was losing his mind.

"Don't look at me like that, old woman! I won't have you casting evil looks at me! And you!" He turned his anger on Tulip. "You lying strumpet, playing with my emotions, pretending you love me when clearly you do not!"

Tulip gasped and melted into tears at once, hardly able to speak.

"That's not true! I do love you!"

The Prince's face was ashen, his eyes sunken and dark with illness, his anger growing with every word.

"If you loved me, truly loved me, then none of this would be happening! Mrs Potts and Cogsworth would still be here! The animals in the maze wouldn't have attacked me, and I wouldn't look like this! Look at me! Every day I grow uglier and more wretched."

Nanny put her arm round Tulip, who was crying so hard she couldn't breathe properly, let alone say anything in her defence. Though even if she had, he wouldn't have heard her; his anger was growing completely out of control.

"I can't stand the sight of you! I want you out of my castle this moment! Don't bother packing your things."

He rushed to the ladies, grasped Tulip by the hair, and pulled her towards the door, knocking over Nanny in the process.

"I won't have you in the castle another moment, do you understand? You disgust me!"

Tulip was weeping harder than ever, screaming for the Prince to let her go so she could see to her nanny, when Gaston came into the room.

"What on earth is going on here, man?"

He wrenched Tulip from the Prince's clutches and helped Nanny to her feet.

"What are you playing at, sir? Are you deranged?" Then, turning his attention to the ladies, he said, "Go to your rooms, ladies, I will take care of this."

The ladies waited in their rooms with their bags hastily packed. They had no idea what to think of the entire matter. Clearly the Prince was suffering from some sort of fever from his wounds and exhaustion. They sat in silence until Lumiere came into the room. His face looked grieved.

"Princess, I see you have packed your things. If you and Nanny could follow me, I will escort you to your carriage." He could see the numerous questions written on Tulip's face. "We think it's best you go home to your mother and father. The Prince will write you when he is feeling, more ... like himself again."

Nanny spoke. "Yes, I think that is best. Come now, child, all will be well. I promise."

And the ladies walked through the castle and into the courtyard to meet the carriage with as much dignity and composure as they could gather in light of their terrible ordeal.

CHAPTER XIV

THE DESCENT

The princess never heard from the Prince again. The Prince had stopped raging on about spells and evil curses; he saw how they had looked at him when he did. They thought he was mad. He couldn't blame them. He often thought himself mad. He almost wished he were. He had taken to staying indoors since he had chased Tulip out of the castle. He never left his room, didn't allow the servants to open the curtains, and lit only one candle in the evenings, saying the doctor advised it for his recovery. The only visitor allowed was Gaston.

"You're sure this is how you'd like to handle this, Prince?"

The Prince did his level best not to slip into one of the fits of rage that seemed to seize him so easily these days.

"I am quite sure, my friend. It's the only way. You're to ride out to Morningstar Castle to officially break off the engagement."

"And what of the marriage settlement? The king will be destitute without your promised arrangement."

The Prince smiled. "I'm sure he will. But that is what he deserves for flinging his stupid daughter at me! She never loved me, Gaston! Never! It was all lies! All a means to get to my money, for herself and her father's kingdom!"

Gaston saw he was getting worked up. He didn't bother arguing that he thought Tulip actually did love him. He had tried convincing him of that in the first few weeks of his breakdown. But nothing Gaston said convinced him. Something must have happened that day in the hedge maze to make the Prince believe Tulip didn't love him, and there was nothing anyone could say to convince him of the contrary.

Whatever it was, Gaston had to trust that his friend was right. Tulip might have been playing him for a fool all along. Frankly, Gaston didn't think she was smart enough to play such a clever trick; he hadn't marked her as a mercenary. He had thought he'd chosen wisely when he had originally made the match, and now he felt sorry for the trouble it had caused.

"I will ride out this day, my good friend. You just rest."

The Prince smiled a wicked smile that distorted his face in the vague candlelight, casting villainous shadows. It almost made Gaston feel frightened of his friend.

CHAPTER XV

THE HUNT

The Prince hadn't left his rooms for months; he was held captive by his fear and anger, which were mounting by the day. The only servant he now saw was Lumiere, and he was rather oblique on matters of the household when the Prince enquired. He stood there holding a small gold candelabrum, making sure not to cast light on his master's face, or his own, for fear of showing the pure terror he was trying to conceal while looking at the Prince's form.

The Prince looked ghastly, pale and worn. His eyes were like black pits and his features were becoming more animal than human. Lumiere hadn't the heart to tell the Prince that everyone else in the castle had become enchanted after he broke Tulip's heart. It became clear to Lumiere that the Prince did not see the servants as they saw themselves. Whatever he saw was horrifying. He kept going on about statues moving about the castle, casting their eyes in his direction when he wasn't looking.

Lumiere and the other servants saw nothing of the sort, and not a single person on staff wished the Prince harm. Lumiere knew it was only a matter of time before he, too, was transformed into some household object like the others, and then his master would be left alone with only the horrors that were conjured in his mind.

Lumiere wished there was another way; he wished the Prince hadn't taken this path, dragging the entire household along with him into darkness. How he missed the young man the Prince had once been, before cruelty overtook him and besmirched his heart.

Mrs Potts had reminded them with stories of what a promising young man he had once been, and Cogsworth still held faith the Prince would change his heart and break the curse; they all did.

In the meantime, it was up to Lumiere to take care of him as long as he could.

"Won't you please go outside, Prince? You are withering indoors. You need to see the sun and breathe fresh air!"

The Prince dreaded the idea of anyone seeing him as he was. After the ruin of Tulip's family, his malformation progressed beyond his wildest fears.

He looked like a monster.

Like a beast.

Clearly there was nothing he could do to break the curse; the sisters had lied. They had never intended for him to be able to break the curse; all his efforts with Tulip were in vain.

Lumiere was still standing there, waiting for his answer. The Prince was only reminded of that when he heard the man clear his throat.

"Yes, man, I heard you! I will go outside but not until nightfall! And I don't want anyone lurking in the halls to catch sight of me, do you understand? I don't want to see a single soul! If someone is afoot, they are to avert their gaze from me!"

Lumiere nodded in understanding.

"Shall I arrange dinner in the main dining hall, sir? It's been some time since we've had the opportunity to serve you at tableside."

The Prince felt sickened at the thought.

"We shall see! Now go! I want to be alone."

Lumiere left the room, stopping in the hall to speak to someone. The Prince got himself out of bed for the first time in weeks. His body ached and was stiff – so stiff he found it surprisingly hard to make his way to the door. But the voice sounded like Cogsworth's, and he desperately wanted to see him. When he opened the door, he expected to find the two men talking, but only found Lumiere.

"What is going on here? I heard you speaking to someone!"

Lumiere turned round in fright.

"Only to myself, while I was winding this clock, sir. I'm sorry to disturb you!"

The Prince was losing his temper again, spiralling into a dangerous rage.

"Balderdash! I heard Cogsworth's voice!"

Lumiere looked sad at the mention of his name, but the Prince persisted. "You mean to tell me you weren't speaking to him? You haven't seen him at all?"

Lumiere, still holding his brass candlestick, calmly replied, "I can say with all honesty, sir, it has been some time since I've seen dear Cogsworth in the flesh."

CHAPTER XVI

THE SUN GOES DOWN

Twilight was his favourite time, the in-between time when everything looked perfect and anything was possible, especially in spring. The darkening sky was lilac, making the moon all the more striking.

The Prince did feel better being outdoors, and Lumiere had made good on his promise. The Prince hadn't seen a single person while making his way out of the castle. Though he couldn't help feeling fearful someone could come upon him at any time. He decided a walk in the woods would be best. Once there, he felt more at ease. It was darker now, and the canopy of trees overhead obscured the light almost entirely except for little patches revealing a star-filled blanket of night. He had always seen well in the dark, but since he'd been in seclusion for so long, his eyes were even keener in darkness than before. He did feel quite beastly, actually, like a creature prowling in the forest.

Prowling.

Yes, that was exactly what he was doing, and he liked it. He almost felt more at home here than he did in his chamber. At times he felt like he couldn't breathe in his room, just sitting there, waiting for those sisters to swoop upon him like a pack of Gorgons. However, in the forest, everything felt right, somehow perfect, like home. Though he wasn't sure if that, too, was the lure of the witches. If they had somehow enchanted the forest to draw him in, make him feel more natural there, trap him in surroundings that would increase his beastliness. He suddenly wanted to flee home, to shut himself away, but something caught his ear.

He quickly hid behind a very large, moss-covered tree stump to see what was coming. It was Gaston with his hunting rifle, but before the Prince could react, shots rained upon him, penetrating the tree trunk, splintering the wood and sending his heart into a manic rhythm he thought would kill him.

Something other than fear was growing inside him, something terrible and dark that obscured his fondness for, and even made him forget, his friend. Indeed, for a moment, this beast couldn't recall Gaston. There was some recollection, but nothing he could put his finger on. Then he remembered.

He felt different, like he was slipping into a deep, dark ocean; he felt himself drowning in it, losing himself completely while something else took over, something that felt alien yet familiar and comfortable at the same time.

Everything in his periphery narrowed, and the only thing he could focus on was Gaston. Nothing else existed; nothing else mattered but the sound of blood rushing to Gaston's beating heart. The sound enveloped him, matching his own heartbeat. He wanted Gaston's blood. He wasn't even aware that he rushed forward, knocking Gaston over and pinning him to the ground.

His own power frightened him; it was so easy to take a man down, to hold him there, rendering him defenceless. He wanted nothing more than to taste his warm, salty blood. But then he looked into Gaston's eyes and saw fear. And he again recognized his friend.

Gaston was frightened. The Prince had not seen him look fearful since they were young boys.

He had been about to take the life of his best friend. A man who had saved his own when they were boys. He snatched Gaston's gun from his shaking hands and flung it far into the woods. He ran as fast as he could, leaving Gaston confused and alone and wondering what sort of foul beast had attacked him. He could only hope Gaston didn't know it was his old friend the Prince.

CHAPTER XVII

THE PRINCE IN EXILE

The Prince didn't leave his rooms after that night in the woods. He heard the commotion downstairs when Gaston burst into the castle, seeking help with his wounds. The Prince wanted to help his friend but knew Lumiere had it well in hand. The doctor was called, Gaston's wounds were attended to, and excuses were made for the Prince's absence.

"How did you explain the state of the castle?" the Prince asked Lumiere later, wondering how things must have looked to Gaston.

But it might not have mattered to Gaston – who, like the Prince, appeared to be losing recollection of the Prince's former life. In fact, even the court was losing any awareness of Gaston, the Prince and, in some cases, their own lives before the cursed transformation.

"A man came to the castle. A stranger, but so familiar," Lumiere had said, referring to Gaston. "He had been attacked in the forest nearby while hunting. And he apologized for intruding on a royal court, but needed help. He was mortally wounded."

"This man," the Prince said, "had he any idea what attacked him in the forest?"

"A beast, sir, that is what he said, some sort of animal. But like none he'd ever seen before."

Animal.

Beast.

Weren't those the words the witches used? The exact words? Those women were probably dancing with joy, chanting and clicking the awful heels of their stupid little boots.

"Sir," Lumiere croaked, "might I suggest saying you prefer the castle to be left unoccupied and kept for you by the groundskeeper?"

"Have we a groundskeeper?" asked the Prince, once again struggling for recollection.

"Yes, sir. Not in the traditional sense, but yes. We have everything. Everyone is here, sir, you just don't see them. Your every wish will still be attended to."

Lumiere looked lost in thought for a moment while the Prince waited for him to continue.

"And I don't know, sir, how long you will have me as a companion. I don't know what will become of me when the curse takes its effects. But I will still be here like the rest, I'm sure of that. We will all do our best to make ourselves known to you when we can. To let you know you're not alone."

The Prince didn't know what to say.

"We just hope you're able to break the curse."

Something snapped in his mind; his eyes were wild and he verged on the edge of frenzy. *Break the curse! He hopes I'm able to break the curse!*

"As if there was a moment that went by that I thought of anything else but breaking this accursed spell! Get out of here before I strike you!"

Lumiere backed away with every spiteful word.

"I'm sorry, sir! I didn't...."

The Beast Within

"Get out now!" And that was the last the Prince, now the Beast, saw of Lumiere.

CHAPTER XVIII

THE ODD SISTERS' SPY

At the top of a grassy hill was a dark green gingerbread-style mansion trimmed with gold and with black shutters. Its roof stretched skyward, its shape resembling a tall witch's cap. Nestled within the house were the odd sisters, having their morning tea. Martha was bringing in a tray of hot blueberry scones when she heard Lucinda squeal with delight.

"She's here! She's here!"

All the sisters ran to the window, tripping over themselves to see who was there. She walked up the dirt path. Her beautiful golden eyes, lined in black, shined with little specks of green in the morning light as she made her way to the front door.

Martha was there to greet her.

"Pflanze, hello! Ruby, quick, get her a saucer of milk!"

Pflanze walked in calmly among the frenzied squeals of excitement that surrounded her. She took her customary seat at the kitchen table, where her saucer of milk was already waiting for her.

Lucinda spoke first. "We've seen everything, Pflanze." She was shaking with delight; she was so excited!

"Yes, everything! We've seen it all!" said Ruby. "You've done well, our beloved!" They surrounded her, chattering away like little birds while she drank her milk. The heels of their boots were making a clicking sound on the wood floor as they sang Pflanze's praises.

Circe came into the room bleary-eyed to see why her sisters were in such a tizzy at that early hour.

"Ah, I see, Pflanze has finally come home!" She stroked Pflanze on the head as she finished her milk.

"And where did you get off to, pretty girl?"

Circe's older sisters looked at each other fearfully, which only succeeded in making them look guilty.

It was rare Circe let them get away with their small deceptions. They found it very hard to keep secrets from their little sister. They were often up to some sort of skulduggery, anyway, so it wasn't a stretch when she'd ask what they'd been doing. It was almost as if they liked being caught by her.

"Or perhaps I should be asking you ladies what you've been doing?"

Lucinda put on the most innocent face she could conjure, but it didn't fool Circe. "Oh, don't try pulling that with me, Lucinda! I know when you've been up to your trickery. Now out with it!"

Pflanze looked up at the witches, all four of them, blinked slowly in thanks for the milk, adjusted her paws, and jumped down from the table. She was above such conversations. She curled up in front of the fireplace while the sisters had it out.

"So?" Circe had her hand on her hip, waiting for her older sisters to answer.

"Pflanze has been with the Prince, keeping an eye on him for us, that's all."

Circe rolled her eyes.

"I told you not to meddle with him. I told you to leave him alone!"

Martha almost knocked over the teapot in protest. "We haven't meddled, I promise! We've just been looking in on him."

Circe couldn't help asking, "And what did you see?" but she knew the moment she asked it was a mistake. The words rained down on her like a storm; she got caught in the flurry of their fragmented stories that they were all too pleased to share.

"Oh, we've seen everything!" "Nasty, terrible things!" "Worse than we imagined!" "Murder!" "Lies!" "He drove a girl to suicide!" "She jumped off the cliffs!" "Ugly, nasty, horrible beast!" "Broken hearts, romancing tarts!" "Ah, are we rhyming now? Lovely!"

Circe put an end to it before the rhyming continued. "No, no you're not! No rhyming!"

Much like everyone else, Circe found it hard to follow her sisters when they got excited. You'd think after almost 20 years of living with them it would get easier, but as the years passed, their mania just made Circe's head spin more.

"Sisters, please, just one of you speak, and please tell it slowly and in a straight line."

The three witches were stone silent.

"I know you are capable of speaking normally, I've heard you do it! Please."

Ruby spoke. "He's turned into the Beast, as we thought he would. He almost killed Gaston while stalking in the forest."

Circe looked disappointed. "But he didn't kill him, so there's still hope?"

Lucinda's already pinched lips puckered even smaller. You could always tell how angry she was by how small her lips became.

"You still love him, don't you?"

Circe walked away from her sisters and sat on the chair next to the fireplace to be near Pflanze.

"I wish you could talk, dear Pflanze," said Circe with a sigh. I wish you could tell me what happened so I wouldn't have to suffer these lunatic sisters of mine!"

Martha chucked her teacup at the wall in frustration. "How dare you!"

Ruby had tears flowing from her eyes. "I never thought to hear such words from you, little sister, not after everything we've done for you!"

Circe put an end to the theatrics at once. "Just stop! All of you! Stop! I'm sorry. I didn't mean it; it's just sometimes you do drive me to distraction! Of course I'm not in love with him; I had just hoped he would have learned his lesson by now. Changed his ways and made a better life for himself!"

Lucinda smiled at her little sister. "Of course, dear, you always cared about people. Sometimes we forget that we are not alike. We care only for you. We love you for your compassion; we just do not share it."

Circe didn't understand her sisters. They lived in a world logical only to them, with their own twisted moral code. Often what they said made sense to her intellectually; other times their words simply confused her. This made her thankful for her capacity for compassion. Without it, she felt, she would be just like her older sisters.

"It's hard to feel sorry for those willing to fling themselves into disaster. They are their own undoing, my dear. They bring it upon themselves. They don't merit your pity."

Circe sighed, because she knew there was logic in her sister's argument; there was just no heart. They sat to tea, chatting about everything the Prince had done since she had last seen him, this time more calmly.

"He thought he could break the curse with poor Tulip, and she really did love him, adored him! But he blamed her when their kiss did not break the curse! Of course he didn't love her. Not really. Not true love. She loved him, true! But the curse dictates both given and received! He thought his selfish version of love would fool us, and he broke her heart in the process!"

Circe felt horrible for what had happened to Princess Tulip, and resigned herself to making things right for her and her family. Lucinda saw in Circe's face that she felt guilty.

"The Prince did that to her, Circe, not you!"

Circe sighed. "I know, but he destroyed her and her family trying to break the curse! My curse!"

Martha smiled at her little sister. "The old queen blighted the land and left a trail of disaster and death in her wake. Should we blame ourselves?"

Ruby laughed. "Oh, how she would have hated to be called the old queen! But that is what she has become so many years after her death: she's become the old queen of legend and myth! But we know the truth! We know she was real! The queen who ruined herself over grief and vanity."

Lucinda joined in the laughter. "Oh, she would have hated that name indeed! She would fling curses, and threaten to kill anyone who referred to her as such! But she's dead now! Dead, dead, dead! Fallen off the rocky cliffs!"

Circe remembered Tulip.

"So, it was she – Tulip – who was driven to suicide? Who threw herself off the cliffs?" Circe asked.

"Oh, I think she did for the loss of her daughter and of herself. She drowned in her own misery and regret in the end. I almost felt sorry for her."

Circe wondered how many stories like this she hadn't heard from her sisters. It was clear they were not speaking of Tulip, but some queen who had thrown herself from a cliff.

"No, I meant Tulip. Your words led me to believe she'd thrown herself off the cliffs of her father's shores."

Lucinda answered, "She did, my dear, but was saved by our friend Ursula."

Circe glared at her sisters. "And what did the sea witch demand in return?"

Ruby looked hurt. "You think so little of the company we keep?"

Lucinda added, "And how would we know what Ursula took from her? We are not privy to the goings-on in every kingdom!"

Circe gave her sister a look as if she knew very well that was a lie, and her sister relented, as they often did with their Circe. She was their one weakness. "She took nothing from her she actually needed."

Circe didn't look convinced. "I want you to make it right with Ursula! You give her something in exchange for whatever she took from Tulip! And I am going to sort out the kingdom's affairs!"

Lucinda looked deeply unhappy. "If you insist."

Circe narrowed her eyes. "I do! And, Sisters, we're to see that Tulip's beauty is returned to her without delay!"

Ruby was surprised their little sister had guessed what the sea witch had swapped for Tulip's life.

Circe smiled smugly. "Don't look so surprised! Ursula's beauty was ripped from her years ago, so it would stand to reason she would try to regain it by devious means! I think it's terrible what happened to her, but it doesn't excuse her actions!"

Lucinda spoke. "Doesn't it? Someone has stolen her beauty and absconded with her true voice. Her losses are too many to count. So much was taken from her and then scattered across the vast ocean so she may never find it again – and for what? A trifle!"

Circe rolled her eyes at her sisters again. "Ursula's deeds were not trifles!"

Lucinda continued. "Whatever our differing opinions may be, I will do what you ask because I love you far too much to watch you suffer and blame yourself for Tulip's unhappiness."

Martha looked panicked. "But what will we give her? Nothing too precious, nothing from the vault!"

Ruby was also in a panic over the thought of giving something away to Ursula. "Circe would have us give away all our treasures! First one of our enchanted mirrors, now what?"

Lucinda, who seemed unusually calm, quelled Martha's fears. "Don't worry, we won't part with anything too precious. I promise."

Then she looked to Circe. "I assume you will be off to Morningstar Castle straight away?"

Circe had in fact decided she would venture out there right away.

"Yes, I will."

Lucinda went to the pantry and pushed a few things about until she found what she was looking for: a little velvet drawstring bag.

"When you get there, go to the cliffs and give Ursula this. She will be waiting for you." And she added, "Tulip's beauty will be returned."

Circe smiled, transforming herself from her just-awoken dishevelled state to one that was more presentable for a journey to Morningstar Kingdom. "I'll be off, then. Don't get into any trouble while I'm away. It may be some time before I return."

CHAPTER XIX

THE WOLVES IN
THE WOODS

The Beast woke on the floor in a room he seldom visited. It was dark except for the pink glow of the enchanted rose the sisters had given him on the night of the curse so long ago; its light was hazy under the protective glass dome that covered it, and its petals were few. His anger and anxiety seemed to have subsided after overhearing Belle refusing to dine with him. The maelstrom of his life had finally stopped spinning in his head, and he was able to focus on the present. The present. Belle. How long had she been here?

He could hear her in the hall. She was in the West Wing! She knew it was forbidden. He had told her so! It sounded like she was talking to

Pflanze as they made their way through the wing. Why did women insist on talking to cats as if they understood what they were saying? He could never grasp the concept. He hid behind a changing screen, waiting to see if she was going to enter the room. She did. His heart raced. She was drawn to the rose, spellbound by its beauty. Her curiosity pulled her to it as the Beast's panic rose, triggering his anger to dangerous proportions. He snatched the domed lid from her hands and slammed it back into place, making sure the delicate flower wasn't damaged. His anger raged. All he saw was Belle's terrified face.

"This room is forbidden! Now get out!" She stuttered, trying to find words to defend herself, but her fear took hold of her shaking body and she ran out of the castle and into the forest. She was alone and in despair. She didn't care any longer about her promise to stay in her father's place.

She wanted to leave, to go home. Her father would understand. Together they would find a way to defeat the Beast. She refused to be his prisoner one more night. She ran so far and so deep into the forest she could no longer see the sky overhead; the trees were tall and thick, and obscured every bit of light the moon might have lent. The tree branches looked menacing, like witches' hands seeking her death, and she heard howls in the distance. She was alone and afraid.

The odd sisters laughed and stomped their boots in outright bliss when they saw through Pflanze's eyes what was happening to Belle. The Beast had chased away any hope of breaking the curse. They sang and danced, laughing all the while. "The Beast chased away his chance to break the curse!" "The girl is going to die!"

If Circe were there, she'd want to help the poor girl, but her older sisters had something else entirely in mind. They were quite happy with themselves. They'd thought ahead; they'd thought to keep Circe busy with the sea witch. They'd asked Ursula to keep her there for as long as she could manage. They didn't want their little sister meddling in their plans. Circe didn't embrace death the way her sisters did. She wouldn't approve.

The Wolves in the Woods

Lucinda took a little pouch that was tied to the belt round her impossibly small waist. Inside the pouch was a deep purple powder, which she sprinkled into the fireplace. A terrible black smoke rose from the fire, taking the form of a wolf's head. Its dead shadowy eyes glowed a blazing copper.

Lucinda spoke. "Send the wolves into the wood, scratch and bite until she bleeds, kill the beauty in the wood, make him regret his evil deeds!"

The witches laughed and watched the wolves advance on Belle. They encircled her, growling at her, showing their sharp teeth. They snapped at her, one of them ripping her dress. She screamed.

This time the sisters said the words together: "Send the wolves into the wood, scratch and bite until she bleeds, kill the beauty in the wood, make him regret his evil deeds!"

Belle screamed again, keenly aware she was about to die. There was nothing she could do! She had nothing with which to protect herself. She looked for something, anything, that she could use as a weapon.

The sisters continued their chanting. "Send the wolves into the wood, scratch and bite until she bleeds, kill the beauty in the wood, make him regret his evil deeds!"

The wolves were upon her. How she wished she could see her father just one more time before she died; she couldn't bear to think of him living in a world without her. He would be lost.

"Send the wolves into the wood, scratch and bite until she bleeds, kill the beauty in the wood, make him regret his evil deeds!" The sisters were in a lunatic trance. Lucinda, delving even further into their manic frenzy, changed the chant: "Rip her throat, make her bleed, eat her flesh, my words you'll heed!"

Something flew past Belle – another wolf, she thought, but no, it was enormous. Far too big to be a wolf. She didn't know what was happening. But the sisters saw; they knew what it was.

"Rip her throat, make her bleed, eat her flesh, my words you'll heed!"

The creature was impossibly large and ferocious, with huge talon-like claws and sharp terrible teeth.

Belle was in sheer panic as the sisters' gruesome chant grew louder and more feverish.

"Rip her throat, make her bleed, eat her flesh, my words you'll heed!"

Belle didn't want to die. She'd hardly had a chance to experience life. So far she'd simply read about the many things she'd like to experience, but she hadn't yet had the opportunity to do them. She shut her eyes tightly, trying to be brave, trying not to regret her choices.

"Rip her throat, make her bleed, eat her flesh, my words you'll heed!"

The creature rushed past her, attacking the wolves, killing them all in a bloody slaughter. It all happened so quickly Belle hardly had time to react before it was over. She looked up and saw she was surrounded by blood. The earth was soaked in it; everywhere she looked she saw death. Blood, fur and flesh. It was terrible. What sort of monster could do this? She wanted to run but saw the creature. He looked hurt. The monster that had saved her life was going to die; he was bruised and bleeding, and exhausted from the fight. Her heart went out to him. Something inside Belle told her not to run, told her the creature needed her help.

The sisters watched in shock, realizing their mistake. They should never have sent those wolves to kill Belle. The Beast was chasing her into the woods because he was angry; his rage would have overtaken him and he would have killed her himself. The wolves were a distraction. The wolves were their mistake. The wolves were dead and scattered on the forest floor. The wolves' blood was black and sticky on the creature's paws. The wolves would bring them together.

The witches' only solace was that Belle had seen the Beast for what he was. She had seen the violence he was capable of.

"She will be repulsed by him! Sickened by the death that surrounds him!"

But if any one of us were there, standing near that fire, and could see the looks on the sisters' faces, we would see the sister witches feared the contrary. Why? Because they could see the look on Belle's face.

They could detect her compassion for the Beast. After all, he had just saved her life. The odd sisters decided they needed to take further action.

"It's time to send Pflanze to see Gaston."

"Oh yes, Sister! I'm sure he would like to know where his dearest Belle has got to!"

And Ruby added, "I bet he would, and I am sure if anyone could destroy the Beast, it would be him!"

Chapter XX

The Beauty in the Library

Belle wasn't the sort of girl who got bored easily, but she found herself tired of being trapped indoors. It was too cold to go outside, so she sat idly in the small study next to the fire, wondering when she would see the Beast.

She had grown less cross with him since he had saved her from the wolves, but she couldn't forget why she had run out into the forest, and into danger: his terrible temper. She played the scene in her head over and over. The wolves, the woods, the Beast, the blood. She had almost died that night because of his rage, and why? Because she touched his precious rose? Though her anger and fear hadn't stopped her mending his wounds, had it? She supposed it was the least she could do after he'd saved her life.

Oh, stop this! she thought. She spent far too much time thinking. That was all she did.

Think.

Analyse.

Brood.

She wondered how the women from the stories she loved to read could bear it. Sitting around all day so idle, just waiting to hear the day's news from men. But that was exactly what she was doing now, wasn't it? Waiting for the Beast. There was nothing for her to do in the castle, and she thought she would go mad from the banality. At least at home with Father she had her books, and she could help with his inventions. He needed her. She needed him. She missed him, and she even missed the people from the village.

It was true: everyone in the village thought she was queer for reading so much, and she didn't exactly behave like other girls. So what if she was more interested in reading about princesses than being one herself? She felt thankful her father always gave her the freedom to express herself how she wished and live her life the way she thought was right. He allowed her to be herself. Not many young women had that freedom, and she was starting to understand what a rare and beautiful life she had been living until recently.

Here she was stifled and alone.

The Beast watched her as she sat in the little red chair next to the fireplace.

She didn't know he was standing there. Her face was squished up in disapproval. Like she was reproaching herself inwardly. She was probably scolding herself for mending his wounds, but she couldn't know the truth. How could she?

She didn't know he just as easily could have killed her had the wolves not been there to distract him. Imagine it; imagine if he had killed her. How horrible, how utterly ghastly that he could do such a thing. Another terrible deed added to the long list – a list no doubt being tallied by those witches.

He was sure it would have been the final act of evil that would have pushed his dark heart into further decay, and the witches would be here now to mock him. He would have lost himself completely, if he hadn't already. Surely there was something left of himself. He wasn't entirely a beast now, was he? If he was, wouldn't he have killed her? He wouldn't have cared about breaking the curse. As it was, he needed her desperately. She was his last chance. He wasn't sure if he deserved this chance, but he saw Belle's arrival at the castle as a sign he should try.

How could he possibly make himself love her? Truly fall in love with someone like her? She was nothing like the girls he fancied. She was beautiful, yes, but not in the ways he usually admired. It would never work, and even if he did fall in love with her, how could she ever fall in love with him?

It was hopeless.

He was loathsome.

He saw that now, for the first time. He saw how vile he'd become, and he felt he deserved Circe's punishment.

Perhaps this, right here, was his punishment: never knowing what it was to love.

Belle looked up at him and smiled. He hadn't expected that. "Belle, will you come with me?" She raised one eyebrow and gave him a sly smile like she didn't trust him.

"Okay."

They walked past the vestibule and into a long passageway she hadn't yet seen. It was sparse except for a small red velvet bench and a lonely gargoyle statue, and at the end of the passage was a large arched doorway. When they reached the door, the Beast said, "Belle, there is something I want to show you." He started to open the door but stopped himself. He was surprised by his nervousness.

"But first you have to close your eyes."

She gave him that look again, like she didn't trust him. *Honestly, how could she?* he thought, but she did seem intrigued and slightly more comfortable in his company, which gave him hope.

"It's a surprise!" he said, and she closed her eyes. She could feel the passing of his hand in front of her face to be sure she wasn't peeking. Both of them were so untrusting of each other. He took her by the hands and led her into what seemed like a vast open space. She could tell by the sound her footsteps were making.

"Can I open them?" Her voice echoed. If she hadn't known better, she would have thought perhaps they were in a cathedral.

"No. No. Wait here!" He released her hands. She heard a swish and then felt warm sunlight on her face.

"Now can I open them?" He was actually enjoying this, giving her this gift, and he found himself smiling for the first time in ages.

"All right, now!" he said, and she opened her eyes, which widened at the remarkable sight. "I can't believe it! I've never seen so many books in my entire life!" The Beast hadn't expected to feel this way, hadn't expected what it would mean to him to make someone so happy.

"You ... you like it?" he asked, and she did, more than she could express.

"It's wonderful!" she said, happier than he'd ever seen her before.

"Then it's yours." And he felt something completely unexpected. What had started out as a way to bring them closer together for the sake of breaking the curse turned into something else, something he didn't understand.

He loved making her happy.

"Oh, thank you so much!" Books! Books made her happy. She wasn't like any girl he'd ever known before, and he thought perhaps he liked it. In fact, he was sure he did.

CHAPTER XXI

BEAUTY AND THE BEAST

The odd sisters were in a panic. Even they could see Belle was warming up to the Beast, and the Beast – well, he was experiencing something quite unique to him and utterly terrifying to the witches.

They had to do something.

They had their hands full keeping watch over Belle and the Beast, and now Gaston as well, since they had sent Pflanze to keep an eye on him. They were so consumed they never left the house for fear they'd miss an opportunity to sink their claws further into the Prince's withering heart.

"Just look at them playing in the snow!" hissed Ruby.

"Disgusting!" spat Martha.

"Look at the way she looks at him! Peeking at him coyly from behind that tree! You don't think she's falling in love with him, do you?" screamed Lucinda.

"She couldn't possibly!"

The sisters spent all their time now spying on Belle and the Beast, and with each day their panic grew. It was becoming painfully clear they were falling in love!

"Those damn servants aren't helping. They contrive romance at every opportunity!" cried Ruby.

Ruby, Martha and Lucinda must have looked a mess when Circe returned from her visit to Morningstar Castle. When they heard her come in, the three of them turned as one, startled to see their little sister standing in the doorway. "Oh! Hello!" they said together, looking frightfully tired and rather crazed from long nights of fretting, spying and plotting.

Circe could see something was amiss.

"What is all this?" Circe asked.

Lucinda tried to put on her best face, though having not seen herself in a mirror for several days, she had no idea how frightful she looked. "What do you mean, dear?" she said with a twitch and sputter.

Circe narrowed her eyes, looking as though she was scanning her for some shred of the truth.

"This place! It's a disaster! What on earth have you been up to?"

The odd sisters just stood there. For once they had nothing to say. Lucinda's ringlets were tangled much like a bird's nest, with little bits of dried herbs and candle wax stuck within them, while Ruby's red silk skirt was covered in grey ash and the feathers in her hair were sticking out at even stranger angles than usual, and poor Martha – her face was smudged with some kind of orange powder.

They all stood there before their little sister, acting as if their appearance was as normal as could be – like Circe was stupid or didn't have eyes in her head to see they were up to some sort of trickery.

"Spell-work, I see!" Circe scolded. "You know, whatever you're doing, I've decided I don't want to know! Honestly, I don't feel like dealing with whatever it is! So, is anyone going to ask me how it went with the sea witch?"

Ruby croaked her reply: "And how was it, dear? Did you send our greetings?" Circe gave a start at the sound of her sister's voice but kept her questions about what they'd been doing to herself.

"She's very well, and was quite pleased with the exchange." She went on, "You know, out of all your strange friends I like Ursula best. She's very amusing."

The sisters laughed, croakily, their voices wrecked from their endless chanting.

Circe couldn't keep herself from asking this time, "Seriously, what have you been up to? Look at yourselves. You're a mess, and what happened to your voices? Why are you so hoarse?"

The sisters looked at each other, and with a nod from Lucinda, Ruby took a necklace out of her pocket.

"We got you this!" She dangled the pretty little necklace from her fingertips, swinging it back and forth in an attempt to distract her. It was a beautiful necklace, braided silver with light pink stones.

"Yes! We got you a present, Circe!" said Martha as Circe narrowed her eyes at her scheming sisters.

"Do you think I'm stupid and so easily distracted?"

Martha frowned theatrically. "We thought you would like it! Try it on!"

Lucinda ran towards Circe like an excited little child, her pale face haggard and her red lipstick smudged. "Yes, try it on! I think it will look lovely."

Lucinda went behind Circe to put it round her neck. "Okay, fine! Let's see what it looks like if it will make you happy," Circe said.

And when Lucinda fastened the clasp, Circe slumped into her sister's waiting arms. "That's right, little sister, sleep!" The three witches carried Circe into her room and placed her on the soft featherbed, where she slept blissfully so her sisters could continue their fiendish deeds undisturbed.

"We will wake you when it's over, our sweet little sister, and you will thank us for avenging your broken heart."

"No one hurts our little sister!" *"Shhh! You'll wake her!"* "Nothing will wake her, not until we

take the necklace from her pretty little neck...."
"She won't be angry with us, will she?" "Oh no,
she couldn't be, we're doing this for her own good!"
"Yes, *her own good*!"

CHAPTER XXII

THE ENCHANTED MIRROR

The sisters had seen enough of Belle and the Beast over the past several days to know where this was heading; what with their daily frolics, bird-watching and disgusting looks of tenderness, it was all the sisters could do to keep themselves from retching. If either of them got the nerve to kiss, it would be over. The curse would be broken. Thank Hades Belle and the Beast were each too bashful to make the first move, so for now the witches' curse was safe. What they needed to do was focus their attentions on someone who could rip Belle and the Beast apart before disaster struck – and that was when they had their idea.

They gathered again near the fire, this time tossing in a silver powder that sparked and made a putrid smell.

"Make her miss Father dear, show Belle her greatest fear."

The witches' laughs grew into a cacophonous maelstrom that travelled with the winds to the Beast's enchanted castle, casting an ill omen over the lovers holding hands in the moonlight.

The sisters watched.

"Belle, are you happy here with me?" The Beast's large paws enveloped her little hands as he waited for her answer.

"Yes," she said, turning away.

"What is it?"

She looked heartbroken.

"If only I could see my father again, just for a moment. I miss him so much."

"There is a way," he said.

The sisters watched, holding their breath.

"He's taking her to the West Wing!" Ruby whispered, as if the two lovers could hear her.

"Show her the mirror!" Martha screamed.

"Calm yourself, Sisters. He'll show her the mirror," Lucinda said, smiling, as they watched to see what would happen next.

"Shhh!" Martha hissed. "He's saying something!"

"This mirror can show you anything, anything you wish to see."

The sisters had to cover their mouths to muffle the squeals of glee threatening to burst from their tiny ruby-red lips.

"Take it! Take the mirror!" Lucinda screamed, trying to will Belle into taking the enchanted mirror from the Beast. "She took it!"

"I'd like to see my father, please," Belle said as she looked into the little hand mirror.

The sisters chanted their wicked words once more.

"Make her miss Father dear, show Belle her greatest fear!"

Their cackles echoed across the lands, and along with them, their foul magic. Belle felt a terrible chill. "Oh, Papa! Oh, no! He's sick, maybe dying, and he's all alone."

The Enchanted Mirror

Ruby knocked over the scrying bowl, its water spilling over the gingerbread house's hardwood floors. They could no longer see Belle or the Beast or force their will upon them.

"Martha, quick, get more water!" Martha took the silver bowl and filled it with water, splashing some on her way back to her sisters, who were now on the floor anguishing.

"Here! I have it!" she yelled. "Look! They are starting to appear! What's happening?" Ruby was slamming her fists on the wet floor again and again so violently her hands started to bleed.

"Ruby, stop! She's leaving! She's going to her father! He's released her!"

Ruby's face was streaked with black tears. "But did he give her the mirror? Is she taking it with her? We were unable to finish the incantation!"

Lucinda looked up at her exhausted sisters, worn from long days of witchery. "Not to worry, Sisters, she had the mirror when she left."

Ruby smiled a mischievous grin. "Everything is in place, then. Perfect."

The sisters' odious laughter filled the room as they focused their attentions now on someone who wouldn't need much persuading to commit a bit of chicanery.

CHAPTER XXIII

THE WITCHES' PLOT

Gaston was sitting down to a large banquet in his dining hall, which was heavily decorated with the various animals he'd killed during his many hunting excursions. The chair at the head of the table, at which he was seated, of course, was adorned with elk antlers and draped with animal skins and furs. His cleft chin was jutting out a bit further than usual, which was a manifestation of his extreme good spirits – that is, until the odd sisters clamoured in, disturbing his banquet for one.

"Look here, foul witches! I won't have you popping in and out of my home unannounced!"

"Sorry to disturb your meal, Gaston, but we have news that you might find interesting."

Gaston slammed his knife into his wooden dining table. "First you send that foul, slinking creature to watch over me, and now this! Showing up whenever you desire, to make requests of me, no doubt!"

Ruby twitched her head to the right, about to speak, but it was Martha who defended Pflanze. "She's not here to spy on you, Gaston. She's here to help you."

Gaston's laugh rivalled the witches' own; it filled the hall and reverberated in the witches' ears. "Help me? Help me? Why, I am the strongest, most attractive man in the village!"

The sisters stared blankly at him, wondering if he, or anyone else, really believed that.

"Yes, help you, Gaston. We've found Belle, and she's on her way to her father now."

Gaston fixed his gaze on the witches for the first time since they'd arrived. They had finally got his full attention. Their dresses were deep red, the exact shade of their lips, which were painted to look like a baby doll's. Their raven hair was fashioned in shoulder-length ringlets around their pale faces and adorned with large red plumes. They were painfully thin and looked ludicrous in all their finery, like skeletal beings brought back from the dead to attend a fancy-dress ball.

"You've found Belle?"

"Oh yes, we've found your dearest love!" Ruby sang. "She won't be able to resist you!"

Gaston looked at himself in the reflection of his shiny knife and said, "Well, who can?"

Lucinda grinned, trying not to let Gaston detect her repulsion. "We have arranged some assurances, on the slightest chance *she* can." Gaston raised one brow in curiosity, but Martha continued before he could comment. "We would like you to meet a friend of ours," she said with an evil smile cracking her white face, her make-up causing her to look even more freakishly beautiful. "A very dear friend who we think would be more than happy to help you." Gaston had to wonder what sort of people the witches kept company with. "His name is Monsieur D'Arque. He runs the sanatorium," Lucinda answered, as if she heard his very thoughts.

Gaston wasn't surprised that the sisters were friendly with the rapscallion who ran the sanatorium.

Martha elaborated. "Maurice, Belle's father, has been raving about a beast, has he not? Perhaps the sanatorium is just the place for him." Ruby twittered in delight when she added, "Though I'm sure there would be no need for him to be institutionalized if Belle were to marry you. I'm sure between the two of you Maurice would be well taken care of."

Gaston grasped their meaning instantly, and he was thunderstruck by the brilliance of the idea. He would of course take the credit for it entirely.

"Hmmmm. Poor old Maurice *has* been raving like a lunatic. Why, just the other night he was gibbering incoherently about Belle being captured by a beast."

"See? You would be doing them both a favour if you married Belle. Someone needs to take care of the poor fellow."

CHAPTER XXIV

BELLE'S BETRAYAL

D'Arque was more than happy to comply with Gaston's request to put Maurice into the sanatorium if Belle did not agree to marry him. He knew very well Maurice was just an odd little man who loved only one thing more than his clanking apparatuses, and that was his daughter, Belle.

D'Arque was quite content. His coffers were filled, he had made a new alliance with Gaston and he was about to partake in some good old-fashioned skulduggery.

He was aware of how intimidating he appeared, illuminated by the torchlight, and he loved nothing more than causing fear. Gaston and his mob were gathered in full force in front of Maurice's home. They were a rowdy bunch collected by Gaston from the tavern at closing time. There was nothing quite as menacing as a bunch of hooligans after a long night of drinking, with gold in their pockets and hate in their hearts – all of which, in this case, had been supplied by Gaston. There was little doubt Belle would agree to marry the braggart, and why not marry him? She couldn't possibly do better. Who else in town would have her with all her strange ways?

Belle answered the door, her eyes filled with fear. "May I help you?" she asked.

"I've come to collect your father," said D'Arque. His withered, skull-like face looked evil and horrid in the torchlight.

"My father?" she asked, confused.

"Don't worry, mademoiselle, we'll take good care of him." Belle was seized with fear. She understood when she saw D'Arque's wagon in the distance. They were taking her father to the asylum.

"My father is not crazy!"

In the Beast's small study, where the witches had found him brooding, they watched through Pflanze's eyes everything that was transpiring.

"Look! Look here! She's going to betray you!" said Ruby, but the Beast wouldn't come to the mirror the witches had brought with them so he could see what Pflanze saw.

"She won't betray me, I know it!" The witches' laughter filled the Beast's head, driving him mad.

"She never loved you! How could she?" "She was your prisoner!" "She only pretended to love you so you would let her go!" "How could she ever love someone as loathsome as you?"

The Beast's anger rose to dangerous heights. His roar caused the chandelier to rattle and the room to shake, frightening even the sisters, but Lucinda persisted. "Look! Here's proof if you don't believe us!"

She showed him the mirror. Belle was standing in front of an angry crowd. Holding the enchanted mirror, she screamed, "Show them the Beast!"

His face appeared in the mirror, ugly, frightening and foul, his roar terrifying the mob.

"See! See? She's betrayed you!" Lucinda said as she danced in the Beast's study.

"She never loved you!" screamed Ruby, joining Lucinda in her absurd dance.

"She's always loved Gaston!" chimed in Martha, prancing about like a deranged peacock with her sisters as they taunted the Beast.

"They're to be married the morning after he kills you!" they all sang as they danced in a circle. "It was their plan all along, you see!" They cackled as their dance grew even more repugnant.

The Beast was finally defeated. Completely diminished and heartbroken, he could barely bring himself to meet their gazes when he asked the sisters to leave. "Please leave. You've got what you wanted. I have suffered for hurting your sister. Now, please, I want to be alone."

Lucinda's laugh was more sinister than he'd ever heard it before. "Oh, and you shall be alone! Alone forever, forever a beast!" And the sisters were gone before the sound of their laughter left his draughty study. He was alone and he knew he had brought all this on himself.

Only one thing comforted him: he had finally learned what it was to love. And the feeling was deeper and more meaningful than anything he'd felt before. He felt like he was dying. To die, one must have first been alive. And the Beast could finally say that by finding love, he had lived.

CHAPTER XXV

THE WITCHES' PARTY

The tall green house with black shutters and a witches'-cap roof was silhouetted a little too perfectly against a deep blue twilight, like a paper cutout of a doll's house. Nothing about the witches ever seemed quite real, not even their house. Inside, the witches danced while watching the Beast's demise in the many enchanted mirrors they had placed around their main parlour. They drank honey wine, splashing it on their deep purple dresses, which blossomed about them as they spun in circles, laughing at their own frenzied insanity. They would stop their bacchanalian antics only to mock the Beast and praise themselves for having seen the curse through.

"He's given up!" raved Ruby. "He wants to die!"

Lucinda scoffed. "He's heartbroken, Sisters. He'd rather die than live without that stupid girl!" All three sisters laughed. "Now he knows what it is to be heartbroken!"

The sisters were even more excited to see Gaston's mob arrive. "They're attacking the castle!" The mob would have laid waste to the castle if it weren't for the servants.

"Bloody fools!" screamed Lucinda. "They're trying to defend the fiend!"

Martha spat at the outrageous spectacle between the mob and the servants. "Sister! Don't spit on our treasures!" scolded Ruby, and then she saw a most welcome sight. "Look! Gaston! He's there! They're fighting on the roof!" The sisters stamped their feet, flailing wildly in a manic dance while chanting "Kill the Beast!" over and over. They said it until their voices were raw as they watched the bloody encounter between the old friends, who now were cursed so that they did not remember each other. The Beast didn't even try to fight back.

Gaston was going to kill him, and it seemed the Beast welcomed it, as the sisters had hoped he would.

"Kill him, kill him, kill the Beast!" they yelled, as if Gaston could hear their words, but something changed, something wasn't right. The Beast saw something the sisters could not. Whatever it was gave him the will to fight.

"What is it?" they screamed as they scurried from mirror to mirror, trying to surmise what could possibly have inspired the Beast to fight, and then they saw.

Belle.

That horrible girl, Belle!

"We should have killed her when we had the chance!" Ruby cried.

"We tried!" Lucinda, Ruby and Martha watched as the Beast overpowered Gaston. He had him by the throat, dangling him over the side of the castle.

"Quick, get the scrying bowl!" Lucinda scrambled in the pantry for the oils and herbs they needed for the scrying bowl while Ruby filled the silver bowl with water, and Martha got the egg from the icebox.

The egg floated in the water like a malevolent eye while Ruby tossed in the oils and herbs.

"Make the Beast remember when they were young." Martha and Ruby looked at Lucinda, mouths open.

"What?" Lucinda was panic-stricken.

"That didn't rhyme, Lucinda!"

Lucinda rolled her eyes, vexed. "I don't have time to think of a rhyme! Just say it!" Ruby and Martha looked at each other but didn't repeat the phrase. "What?" Lucinda asked again.

"It's not as fun if it doesn't rhyme."

Lucinda checked the mirrors. The Beast still had Gaston by the neck and was about to drop him. "Sisters, say it with me now if you want to save Gaston!"

Ruby and Martha relented. "Fine! Make the Beast remember when they were young." Their voices were flat and unenthusiastic.

"Say it again!" screamed Lucinda. "Say it louder!"

"Make the Beast remember when they were young!" the sisters screeched.

"Remember when you were boys and he saved your life! Just for a moment, *remember each other*," Lucinda cried. Then, looking at her sisters, she added, "Don't look at me like that! I dare you to do better!"

Ruby was transfixed by something in the mirror nearest her. "Look, it worked, he's letting him go!"

The Beast was bringing Gaston back on to the roof by the scruff of his neck. "Get out!" he growled, tossing Gaston aside. The sisters knew Gaston wouldn't leave. They counted on it.

"Beast!" It was Belle. She was reaching her hand out to him as he climbed up the turret to kiss her.

"No!" wailed the sisters. *"No!"*

But before Lucinda could recite another incantation, her sisters screamed in glee at the sight of Gaston plunging a large knife into the Beast's side. Their delight transmuted into fear, however, when they saw Gaston lose his footing and fall from the castle tower to his death below.

It didn't matter anymore. Gaston didn't matter anymore – not to the witches. He had given them what they wanted; the Beast was dying. He was dying in his lover's arms, heartbroken.

"Let's get Circe! She has to see this!"

CHAPTER XXVI

THE ENCHANTRESS

Lucinda creeped into Circe's room, gazing at her sleeping little sister. She looked so peaceful and beautiful sleeping there. As she unfastened the necklace, Lucinda knew in her heart that Circe would be thankful for what they had done for her.

Circe opened her eyes, then blinked, trying to see which of her sisters was looking down at her with such a mad expression on her face.

"Lucinda." She smiled up at her.

"Circe, we have something to show you. Something very important. Come with me."

Lucinda led her befogged sister to the other room. How it must have looked to Circe, who hadn't been privy to the evening's events. The room was lit by an extravagant number of candles, all of them white and reflecting beautifully in the many enchanted mirrors placed around the space. In the largest mirror she saw the Beast.

"What's this?" she asked as she rushed over to the mirror and placed her hand on its lovely silver frame. "Is he dead?"

All three of her sisters were standing there, hands clasped, like eager little girls waiting for praise. Circe looked down at the scrying bowl, and then back to her sisters. She felt ill, hollow and inhuman.

"You did this?" She thought she was going to be sick. They said nothing. "You killed him?" she cried.

"No! It was Gaston. He killed him!"

Circe couldn't breathe. "With your assistance, I see!" She threw the scrying bowl across the room.

"We thought you would be happy, Circe! We did it for you!"

Circe stared at her sisters in shock. "How could you think I would want this? Look at the girl! She's heartbroken!"

She was looking at Belle in the enchanted mirror.

"I love you," Belle said to the Beast as tears streaked down her face.

Circe was also crying. Her heart was filled with dread and regret. "I never wanted this to happen!" she continued. "Look! She loves him! This isn't fair. I'm bringing him back! I'm giving him a chance to break the curse."

The odd sisters started to scream in protest as they advanced on their little sister, but Circe's fury sent them flying back until they were pinned to the wall.

"Not another word, do you understand?" she snapped. "You say one more word and I will give your voices to the sea witch!"

Lucinda, Ruby and Martha knew their little sister's powers were far greater than their own, but they had always been able to manage her because she was the youngest. It looked now as though that time was past, however. They were too frightened to speak; like broken dolls, they looked inanimate and frozen in their bizarre poses as Circe continued to rail at them. "I'm bringing him back! I'm bringing him back to life, do you understand? If he loves her, too, then the curse will be broken. And you will never seek to reverse it!"

Her sisters hung there, pinned, unable or unwilling to move, not saying a word.

"Never meddle with the Prince or Belle again! If you do, I will make good on my promise! I will give your voices to Ursula and you will never be able to use your foul magic again!" The odd sisters just stared at her, wide-eyed, saying nothing, as they had been commanded.

CHAPTER XXVII

HAPPILY EVER AFTER

Circe put her hand on the face of the mirror where she saw Belle crying over the Beast's dead body. The poor thing thought she had just lost the love of her life.

"Not if I can help it," said Circe as she cast her magic. Rose and silver lights showered down around them, lifting the Beast's body into the air. His body twisted and entangled with the glittering lights until he was no longer the Beast but the man Circe had once known so many years before. The Prince. His face was no longer marred with anger, vanity and cruelty. She could see that his soul had truly changed.

With her magic, Circe encircled the lovers in light that soared up into the sky and cascaded down again, raining beautiful sparks and transforming the castle and everyone within it to their original forms.

"Lumiere! Cogsworth!" cried the Prince, seeing his fondest friends for the first time in many years. "Oh! Mrs Potts! Look at us!"

Circe smiled as she saw how delighted her magic had made the Prince and Belle. They were happy, and they were in love, and they were surrounded by all their friends and family – including Belle's father, who looked more than a little confused suddenly to be at a fancy ball when only moments before he'd been in that appalling sanatorium. But he wasn't going to worry about that just then. He was happy to see his darling Belle again.

It turned out exactly as Circe had hoped it would. With Belle, the Prince had finally learned what it was to love – to truly love and to have that love returned.

She smiled again, taking one last look at the Prince and Belle dancing in the great hall before wiping their image from the enchanted mirror, leaving them to live and love happily ever after.

THE END